D0928757

An unusually cold winter, followed by an unprecedented wet spell, causes a rock-fall in the inner recesses of the dark mountains of Scotland's Central Highlands.

An elderly amateur geologist stumbles on a cave containing the skeletons of a band of Jacobites who had taken refuge there 250 years earlier. With the corpses are the remains of a wooden cask containing thousands of gold coins.

The saga of how these coins, and corpses came to be there follows, a story of loyalty, of comradeship and of courage, ending in tragedy.

The discovery of the gold brings unwelcome publicity to the old and infirm finder of the cave. The media and the politicians are quick to jump on the band-wagon. Then the sinister arrival of a Glasgow thug puts the safety of all the old man holds dear in jeopardy.

the sixth cask

A NOVEL BY
Webster Simpson

ISBN 0 9538690 0 8

Published by
Itelsor Ltd
Trendell House
3 Lintrathen Street, Dundee DD3 8EF
Tel: 01382 825629 Fax: 01382 832316

INVERNESS

✗Culloden

Loch Ness

Loch Arkaig

The Great Glen

The Cairngorns

Loch Oich

Ruthven

Loch Nan Uamh

Loch Lochie

The Monadhliaths

Book 1

Chapter 1
Tuesday 16th April 1996

The old man looked down at the skull. Three things were immediately apparent. First, it was by no means complete. Indeed, the whole lower jaw bone was missing and the back was staved in. But it was a skull, and a human one at that. The second self-evident fact was that whoever it belonged to had been dead for a very long time. The bone was yellowed with age and tending to flake, especially around the shattered rear. Thirdly, it had not been lying where it was for long.

Straightening himself up, old McPherson looked around him. He stood a little insecurely at near the top of a scree slope, under the beetling brows of 250 feet of rugged cliff. The severe winter had brought frosts unprecedented in living memory to the whole of Scotland and to this part of the Highlands in particular. Night after night the temperature had plummeted to minus 20c and lower, even at the much lower levels of Speyside, several miles to the east. Just how cold it had been three or four months ago on this particular mountainside high in the Monadhliaths was any one's guess. It was that exceptional cold, followed in turn by heavy snow, then by a sudden thaw and torrential rain, which had caused a massive land-slide. And it was this land-slide that had brought McPherson to this desolate spot.

McPherson had two passionate interests. History and geology. He had help make history at the Battle of Alemein and then in Normandy all those years ago. Then, for forty-plus years, he had taught it to reluctant scholars at a variety of Scottish schools. His second passion was geology, not a professional interest, but an amateur's indomitable enthusiasm. It was geology that had drawn him deep into these forbidding hills on this particular chilly April morning. The land-slip had carved a great scar across the mountainside, exposing rocks that never before had seen the light of day.

Already, McPherson had found outcrops of cairngorm - that pinkish-blue, semi-precious crystalline stone that gave its name to the massive mountain range many miles away to the east on the other side of the wide Spey valley. Here, hidden in these unfrequented Monadhliaths, the Grey Mountains, were riches to be found by the patient geologist. Cairngorms have no great commercial value, but then McPherson's interest was not financial. It was the sheer magic of finding, recording and photographing the beautiful stones that was his reward.

Below him, scattered down the hundred-foot scree-slope, were the rocks that so recently had been part of cliffs high above where he stood. These were no mere pebbles. Indeed, some were the size of a small house. Below the scree, far down in the glen, the spring sunshine glinted on the smooth surface of a small lochan, the twinkling light bright against the drab back-ground of heather. Beyond that was the backdrop of rolling hills, extending as far as the eye could see.

Dragging his thoughts back to the present, McPherson gazed down again at the skull whose empty eye-sockets so relentlessly returned his gaze. Whose skull? Well, that would be for others to figure out. He would have to tell Constable Grant back at the village. But there was no hurry. The skull had been there for a long, long time and it wasn't going anywhere.

A picture or two might be interesting. He focused his camera and took a couple of shots. Then he started to look around. Where was the rest of the skeleton? If its unfortunate owner had fallen from the crags high above, his body could have been smashed up badly enough. Add to that the work of foxes and scavenging birds and the rest of the remains could be almost anywhere. However, within a few feet, he found more traces of shattered bones. Had it not been for the unmistakable human nature of the skull, no one without considerable medical skill could possibly have identified these shards of bone as human remains. McPherson was puzzled. Why was the skeleton so smashed up? Even a vertical drop of hundreds of feet would not grind the bones like this.

Widening his search, the old man cautiously worked his way up the last few feet of the steep slope to where the scree ended and the cliff began. Apprehensively, he scanned the overhanging rocks that towered above him. Then he looked down. There, at his feet, was a strip of very corroded iron. Carefully, he scraped the stones away from round about it, trying not to disturb the great flakes of rust that encrusted it. He drew a deep breath. A sword! Heavily corroded though it was, the remains of the massive hilt could just be discerned. This was not just any sword. This was a claymore! The massive highland broadsword that had chilled the heart of many a Redcoat in a bygone day.

So the deceased was even more deceased than McPherson had thought. He could only guess at how long these shattered bones had lain here. Easing off his rucksack, he sat down with his back to the rock-face. He did not like mysteries. Who was the dead man? How many years ago had he died?

After a few minutes McPherson struggled to his feet again. It was then he noticed a hole where scree and rockface met. Not a large hole, only about the size of a biggish rabbit burrow. Carefully he enlarged it, scraping at the shale and stones with his geologist's hammer. Suddenly the loose stones cascaded inwards, revealing a cavity two or more feet in diameter. Opening his rucksack, McPherson pulled out his torch. He flashed the beam down the hole. He had found the entrance to a substantial cave whose mouth must have been covered by some earlier land-slide or rock-fall.

The tunnel he had exposed sloped down at nearly forty-five degrees, widening and deepening as it went. The torch light penetrated only ten feet or so and it was impossible to guess how deep the thing was. Dare he venture down? Only a fool would, he told himself. Ah, well, he thought, there is no fool like an old fool! He slipped out of his anorak, dragged his climbing rope from his rucksack and fastened one end round a substantial boulder. Carefully, he tied a bowline on the other end and pulled it over his shoulders to fit loosely under his arms. Feet first, he squirmed into the hole, holding his torch tightly in his left hand and letting the rope slip through his right. After some twenty feet the ground under him began to level out. He stopped his descent, the dust of his downward movement swirling around him. Rolling on to his side, he shone the torch round about him. The roof height was now about five feet. Cautiously, he pulled himself into a crouched position. The cave went deeper still into the mountainside. The air was cold and musty and a wave of claustaphobia swept over him. McPherson felt his chest tighten and found himself increasingly short of breath.

What was surprising was how dry the place was. Most highland caves he had explored in his searches of rock samples were dripping wet. This was not. He shuffled forward another yard or two and found he could now stand upright with a few inches of headroom. Under his feet was solid rock. He turned round and shone the light back to where he had come from. A steep slope of stones and rocks reached up to a small patch of blue sky just visible through the entry hole. Slipping the loop of rope from his shoulders, he turned again and, with the greatest of care, worked his way into the shadows. Suddenly his torch beam lit up another skull, a complete one this time, part of a complete skeleton. Well, not exactly a skeleton, for dried and mummified remains clung to it, with bits of bone sticking out here and there. McPherson took a deep breath. He was no stranger to death and had seen much worse all those years ago under an African sky. Still, it was unnerving. It reminded him all too clearly of the half-burnt, dried-out remains of Allies and Germans alike that he had so often seen scattered in the Sahara sand.

Chapter 2

Once the initial shock at his discovery had passed, he examined the corpse quite clinically. The man had been big, all of six feet and maybe more. Only a few scraps of clothes adhered to the remains and it was impossible to deduce how he had been clad. McPherson raised his torch and its light penetrated farther into the cave. He found his eyes were becoming used to the gloom and that he could see not only what was illuminated directly by the beam but also what the feeble light reflected from floor and ceiling revealed. More skeletons, four, five, six. All part mummified, part skeletal. There were also the rusted remains of several swords and dirks. The black patch on the floor was, no doubt, all that was left of a fire.

Squatting down, McPherson tried to piece together the jigsaw puzzle he saw before him. Six long-dead men with dirks, claymores and, yes, the remains of some antique firearms, the wooden stocks long-since rotted to dust, but the rusty locks and barrels still quite recognisable. Some robber band? Some cattle reivers? Or perhaps Jacobite fugitives from Culloden and the '45? And how had they died? Had they fallen prey to their enemies, whoever they might be? Unlikely, judging by the fact that all six were reclined in death and the swords were gathered in one place indicating there had been no struggle.

No, he thought, by far the most likely scenario was that the unfortunates had been entombed by a rock fall not unlike the recent one. The man whose half-skull had started McPherson's search must have been crushed under the avalanche of rock, there to be interred until that unexpected 1996 resurrection day which had cast at least some of him back into the daylight. Perhaps he had been the lucky one. How long had these other six waited here in darkness for death to find them? The old man shuddered.

The silence was broken by the sound of stones slipping down the gradient at the mouth of the cave. In reality, it was only a whisper of stone on stone, but, to his keyed-up nerves, the sound was like thunder. The tiny hole that was the entrance seemed far, far away above him up a slope that almost felt beyond his ability to climb. The rock walls seemed to close in upon him and he trembled. For a moment he held his breath, cursing himself for venturing into this tomb. Then he steadied himself with a deliberate act of will. A few strides took him to the foot of the slope. Using the rope with an agility remarkable for a man in his late seventies, he squirmed and wriggled his way into the daylight.

For about ten minutes he just sat, blinking in the daylight, his lungs gradually recovering from the foul air below ground. Then from his rucksack he retrieved his Thermos of tea and a handful of biscuits. What should he do now? The very human and sensitive part of him felt the guilt of one who has violated a war grave. The historian in him, however, wanted to record all that could be learnt from his chance discovery. The tired old man wanted to get off home. The historian wanted more details of all that the cave concealed.

The old man dreaded another descent into that horrble tomb. The historian wanted pictures. Eventually, the historian in him won.

He descended again into the darkness, this time complete with camera. He had about twenty-three shots left on the film. Systematically, he worked his way round the cave, his torch propped up to give sufficient light to frame each shot. Then he would close his eyes tightly and press the button, thus not dazzling himself every time the camera flashed. He was more than half-way through when he realised that, in the darkest recesses of the cave, the ground fell away sharply. He swung the torch round and down. On the rock floor some eight feet below where he stood was an untidy heap of debris. Through it shone a dull, golden gleam. Squatting down, he peered through the gloom. His torch beam homed in on a pile on the rock floor below. Gold coins! Dozens of them! The temptation to scramble down was nearly overwhelming. However, the tightness was back in his chest and common-sense told him it was time for him to go up, not farther down. Carefully he focused his camera using the telephoto lens. He took seven snaps.Then he moved back towards the cave mouth, still taking photographs until the whirring noise of the automatic re-wind on the camera told him the film was full.

By no means reluctantly, he scrambled out into the daylight. The pain in his chest was worse than ever. He sat on a flat stone and took slow, deep breaths and the constricting feeling gradually ebbed away. The short Spring day was already nearly over and the watery sun had sunk low in the western sky.

Hurriedly, McPherson dragged four or five biggish rocks over the cave-mouth. He stood up and surveyed his handiwork. No casual passer-by would notice anything, even if there were such a thing as a casual passer-by in this remote spot. He built a little cairn of stones over the half-skull that had first caught his eye, taking care that not one stone actually made contact with the relic. Pulling on his rucksack, McPherson started the long trudge down the scree-slope, across the bog, past the lochan and down the ill-defined sheep-track parallel with the roaring cataract where the swollen burn plunged down a gorge. Eventually, he stumbled on to the place where he had left his car. Long before he reached it, the sun had disappeared and both cold and darkness seemed to descend like a blanket around him.

It was too late to bother the police tonight. Besides, he was not sure that he wanted to. Instinctively, he knew that, as soon as he revealed his discovery to anyone, he would have no peace. The cave would not merely interest historians. Its very existence would flood Speyside with the media, with sight-seers and with every kind of crank imaginable. Furthermore, he really could not face going down that hole into that grave a third time.

Chapter 3

Back at the cottage, McPherson suddenly felt terribly tired, too tired to prepare any supper. Irene, his late wife, would never have let him go to bed unfed, but it was now five years and more since he had followed her coffin into the Kincraig Churchyard. He took a stiff dram of whisky and tumbled into bed, after having kicked off his boots and shuffled out off his anorak.

He slept fitfully, his sleep being punctuated by nightmares featuring mummified bodies, but bodies that did not have the decency to remain dead. Through the night they pursued them, until at last he awoke, exhausted and fevered. He struggled shakily to his feet, hoping he was not going down with something. His chest hurt when he breathed and all his joints ached. Stiffly, he tottered into the tiny kitchen. A cup of tea and a slice of toast, he thought, then he would feel better. It did help but he knew he was far from well.

Somehow, getting his film developed seemed a priority. His hands were strangely shaky as he extracted it from the camera and put in the brightly coloured envelope. The post-box was less than a hundred yards away but he felt positively light-headed when he staggered back in through his front door five minutes later. He flopped down in his chair and was asleep in seconds.

The next few days were a blur. He lacked the energy to go to bed and slept in his chair. At last he realised he was not going to throw whatever it was off easily so, for the first time for years, he telephoned the doctor. It was nearly noon when Dr Park arrived. Although McPherson had not consulted him professionally in years, they were old friends.

"Why did you not call me sooner, you old fool?" demanded the doctor, with that imperious manner which is peculiar to his profession. Then with a rough tenderness and genuine concern, he examined his patient carefully, paying particular attention to his chest and his breathing.

"If I'm not much mistaken, you're developing pneumonia. The sooner we get you to hospital the better. I'll get the ambulance to shift you to Inverness. They'll soon sort you out."

McPherson hated hospitals but was now too sick to quarrel. As they talked, the door-bell rang. The doctor answered it and returned a minute or so later.

"Post," he said, dropping a bulky envelope on McPherson's knee. "Been taking more photos of stones, have you?"

The old man smiled weakly, too tired to bother opening the packet and certainly too tired to explain the subject matter of his pictures. Dr Park left, but not before assuring his patient that he would return in time to help him to the ambulance. McPherson sat staring at the unopened packet on his knee. Why had he taken the wretched pictures? Lingering in that cave to take them was literally likely to be the death of him.

11

Why not put them straight in the bin? However, the historian in him won once again. His discovery was unique and someone ought to be interested.

With an enormous struggle, he found a bit of paper and a large envelope. In nearly illegible writing, he scribbled a note to one of his old pupils, one of the very few who shared his enthusiasm for history.

"Someday I'll explain where I took these. Make whatever use you want to of them."

Then he put the still unopened package of film and prints into the large envelope. By the time he had addressed it, he was just about passing out. The doctor's return awakened him. Pressing the envelope into his hands, McPherson said, "Post this for me, please. I'm sorry I've no stamps but I'll repay you when and if I come home."

"You'll be back all right, you old rogue! I am afraid we're going to have to put up with you for a long time yet," retorted the doctor with a confidence that in his heart of hearts did not feel was remotely justified. Indeed, the elderly patient was only just conscious when he was stretchered on to the ambulance. He was totally comatose on arrival at the hospital in Inverness an hour later.

Book 2

Chapter 1
Wednesday 16th April 1746

The big man lay in the heather, struggling to regain his breath. The immediate cacophony of battle was over. All that remained were the eerie sounds of the aftermath. The haunting moans of severely wounded men and the indescribable shrieks of injured horses, both mingled with the shouts and oaths of the dragoons as they picked their way across the accursed bog that was Culloden Moor, killing with bullet or bayonet the wounded remnant of the Jacobite forces. Prince Charles Edward Stewart had fled, as had those fortunate enough to be still able to run. But everywhere across the dismal bog lay the shattered frames of men and horses. The smell of battle, that inimitable mix of cordite, excrement and gore, drifted on the bitter wind that swept in from the Moray Firth to the north.

Every instinct told big Hamish McPherson it was time to go. It was past time to go. The battle had been fought and lost hours ago when the Duke of Cumberland's artillery had reaped its deadly harvest among thc Jacobite clans - those proud, impatient highlanders who had stood there in the driving sleet waiting for their vacillating Prince to give the order to charge. Neither Hamish nor his cousin, Davie, would have been there at all but for the fact that they had been sent by their chief, Ewan McPherson, with a message to Cameron

13

of Lochiel. The main McPherson force had been diverted to Blair Atholl by the Prince and had thus not fought at the fateful Culloden battle. So it came about that the two McPherson cousins had found themselves in the battle line, shoulder to shoulder with Cameron clansmen, the sole representatives of their own clan on that disastrous field.

Hamish could have been five miles away and more by now, instead of still within ear-shot of the Duke's butchering dragoons, but only if he were willing to abandon Davie who lay beside him in the heather, uncomplaining, despite both legs being shattered by grape-shot.

"Go, man, go!" Davie urged his cousin. "I'm done for, but you can still make it."

"We'll both beat them yet," hissed Hamish, peering circumspectly though the clump of heather that concealed them from the searching troopers. "They're chasing our lads westward. If we can work our way to the south-east, maybe we'll make it to Moy. That's Macintosh land and surely we'll get some help there."

A moment or two later, a violent squall of sleet obliterated the dismal sight of heartless slaughter to the north. Not wasting a moment, the big highlander scrambled to his feet. Without apparent effort he slung his uncomplaining cousin over his shoulder and set off at a steady six miles an hour. He picked his way through the peat hags and slowly gained height, always following the line of the small burns that drained the higher slopes and at the same time provided some cover. Pausing for breath, he looked back at the scene of the battle in the now distant valley below. The squall, and the cover it provided, had passed. To the west, he could see scattered groups of the broken Jacobite forces trying to put distance between themselves and the marauding victors of today's disaster. Then Hamish saw a detachment of dragoons fan out in good order, clearly bent on the pursuit of the fleeing clansmen. The soldiers set out westwards and then swung south, bringing them dangerously near Hamish's planned line of retreat.

"Time to go!" he muttered, as much to himself as to his kinsman.

Scooping up his charge once more, he set off at a fast stumbling gait. He was now nearly 2000 feet above sea level, gambling that the troopers would expect fugitives to seek shelter among the birches and juniper down in the valleys and glens rather than risk spending the approaching night on the bleak wind-swept hill-tops. The gamble nearly paid off, but, in the deepening dusk, he all but blundered into a score or more dragoons who had scattered and largely slaughtered an exhausted group of clansmen, many of whom might well have been clean away had not ties of blood and kinship led them to carry their wounded with them. Now the dragoons were re-forming. It did not take a great military mind to see what their next move would be - a systematic sweep through the hags and the heather, finishing off with sword or bullet. Ducking down, Hamish dropped Davie as gently as he could beside a hideously butchered highlander.

"For any sake lie still whatever happens," he whispered.

Then he dragged the poor, disembowelled clansman's body over his prostrate cousin, flinching as he pulled a yard or more of intestine over the dead and the living alike to complete the camouflage. Easing himself up on his knees, he watched the assembling line of troopers. Barely a couple of hundred yards away; not much time left. Wriggling forward on his belly, he squirmed his way down into a peaty hollow that had ten or more inches of deep brown water covering an unknown depth of inky black mud. Hoping it was deep enough to cover him but not so deep as to swallow him up completely, he hacked off a large clump of heather with his dirk, gripped the stem of the clump firmly in his teeth and lowered himself into the breathtakingly cold mix of water and mire. Now he must hope that no sharp eyed dragoon would wonder why a lone bunch of heather grew in a peat-bog.

After what seemed hours, but was in truth less than thirty minutes, the hideous sounds of murder ceased. The screams of the dying, the gunshots and the clink of the horses' harness one by one died away and a deep stillness, broken only by the whistle of the wind in the heather, fell on the moor. Hamish eased his head round so that one ear was out of the water. He then started counting, and only when he had counted to one thousand without hearing anything of his foes, he very cautiously raised his head out of the mud. Then, bit by bit, he pulled himself onto the relatively dry moorland. Darkness was falling fast, but he could still discern the enemy, now nearly a mile away, heading northwards for Inverness.

"Thank God you've come," breathed Davie, as Hamish hauled the now-stiffening body off him.

"Let's go," said Hamish. "We'll make Moy yet and then there will be friends aplenty."

After a nightmare stumble through the growing night they did reach Macintosh land, although not the great house of Moy itself. Chilled to the bone and utterly exhausted, they reached an outlying barn and cottage where kind hands dressed as best they could Davie's terribly mangled legs.

Dry straw was provided while their plaids which had been stained with peat and blood were roughly washed and then dried over a smoky peat fire. Within minutes, Hamish slipped into a fitful sleep.

Chapter 2

It was still dark when urgent hands roused him from sleep. The news from every quarter was bad, he was told. Cumberland's victorious army was harrying not only the survivors of the battle. There were reliable accounts of men who had declared themselves neither for one side nor the other being killed where they worked in their fields. Nor did the carnage stop there. School lads from Inverness who had skipped their lessons in order to watch the fighting had been overtaken in the rout and were either run through or shot down where they were, on the Culloden to Inverness road. Women and children had been dragged from their hovels and bayoneted or clubbed to death, all on the pretext that they might have given succour to the fleeing wounded of the fray.

The anxious hosts had done what they could for the two cousins. Now they were fretting that the pair should take the road south even before daylight so as to put as many miles as possible between themselves and the avenging Redcoats. After a minimal breakfast of oatmeal and water, they set out, accompanied for the first five miles by two strong men of the Macintosh clan. These helped greatly, sharing in the work of carrying the semi-conscious Davie. The word was that the remnants of the Jacobite army were to re-group at

Ruthven, some thirty miles to the south, deep in Badenoch country in the lands of the McPherson. Hamish, being a McPherson himself, owed allegiance to the redoubtable chief, Ewan McPherson, known to all by the name of his castle, Cluny, in accordance with the usual Scottish practice of giving a chief the name of his house or lands. Hamish was honour-bound to report to his Chief as soon as possible and therefore was anxious to cover the ground as fast as he could. Although he was a tall, powerfully-built man of twenty, however, there was a limit to what even his strong frame could endure. South of the clachan of Aviemore he had to give up for the night.

Unsure of the welcome he might get and not wanting to bring danger to any innocent family, he skirted round each cottage and farmstead. If anyone tending the black cattle or working in the fields or woodlands saw him, they gave no sign. At length, using the last reserves of his strength, he hacked down a few branches from the plentiful gorse and juniper bushes and fashioned a crude shelter under a rocky out-crop. It was bitterly cold and driving squalls of sleet and rain swept across the broad strath of the Spey. He dare not light a fire, although he had both flint and tinder. Supper was again a handful of oatmeal washed down with water from the burn. As the mixture settled in their stomachs, the coarse-ground grain would swell, giving a comforting illusion of a substantial meal out of all proportion to the nutritional value of the uncooked oats. Only sheer exhaustion enabled them to sleep at all. Huddled together for warmth and with their plaids wrapped around them as many times as the long length of cloth would allow, the two shivered and slept until dawn broke.

Daylight brought better weather and the promise of at least some Spring sunshine. This was an undoubtedly mixed blessing. The visibility was superb, a serious handicap for the fugitives and a considerable blessing to the hunters. Feeling very vulnerable on the open hillside, Hamish decided to leave Davie in the relative safety of their poor shelter and to press on to Ruthven alone. He would make twice the speed and, if he did fall foul of dragoons, his chances of escaping their clutches were infinitely better than if he were encumbered by his wounded kinsman. Furthermore he was desperate to learn what was going on at Ruthven and whether the Prince and his officers were planning a counter offensive. If they were, he would be with them, but only after delivering Davie safely to his kin.

The eight miles to Ruthven proved uneventful. On the east side of the sluggish waters of the Spey the military barracks were starkly silhouetted against the sky. These ugly buildings had been erected on the site of a much earlier stronghold at the top of a steep-sided hillock in a commanding position overlooking the boggy valley of the Spey. The small Government garrison had successfully repelled a Jacobite assault the year before, but the barracks had eventually been taken by the Prince's men. Hamish forded the swollen waters of the Spey with only little difficulty and cautiously approached. He was still some three hundred yards to the north of the rising ground when he was challenged by five highlanders who appeared as if from nowhere, both in front of and behind him. However this was home territory for a McPherson and he was instantly recognised.

Chapter 3

It emerged that a substantial group of the Prince's shattered forces had straggled south to Ruthven in the aftermath of the debacle at Culloden. Principle among them were Ewan McPherson of Cluny and Lord George Murray of Atholl. There had been a council of war which had lasted most of the night. Some were for continuing the struggle. Others, faced with a message from the Prince that the army should disperse, were of a different opinion. The up-shot was the decision that the rank and file should return to their homes and their glens. The leaders and senior officers would no doubt have a price on their heads and most were planning flight to France.

There was understandable bitterness, many murmuring that the outcome would have been very different if Murray had been allowed to command. He was by far the most experienced leader on the Jacobite side and was indisputably the author of the victories at Prestonpans and Falkirk. However, despite Murray holding the rank of Lt-General, Prince Charles had insisted on personally commanding the entire highland army at Culloden, totally disregarding the advice of Murray and other officers whose combat experience dwarfed his own. Murray, himself very bitter at what he knew to be the unnecessary slaughter inflicted on the clansmen in the battle, let it be known that he would write to the fugitive Prince, resigning his commission and stating his intention to return to Atholl and from there to France.

Hamish was ushered into the presence of his clan chief. Ewan McPherson, known universally as 'Cluny' after his lands, looked desperately tired. Cluny's clothes were stilled stained with blood, some clearly his own, as crude bandages on his arm and round his head proclaimed.

"Aye, aye, young Hamish. I hear you did well, but it was a hard, hard fight. I'm proud there were McPhersons there, even if only two of you," said the older man. "We were not able to make it to Culloden in time. Whether our lads would have tipped the balance, who can tell? I was caught up in a skirmish with a troop of dragoons yesterday. We saw them off, but not without cost. I'm taking to the hills, for they'll soon be at Cluny Castle in strength and we'll never hold them. When you've fed, you can head off to Cluny and help hide whatever of the contents we can shift. No doubt they'll burn the place to the ground and there's nothing we can do to stop them, but we can perhaps save our lives yet."

The pessimism and the realism of this assessment of the situation were depressing in the extreme.

"Is it really that bad?' asked Hamish, "I know we took a terrible mauling up there on the moor, but can we not re-group and keep on the struggle until help comes from France?"

"France is full of promises but, when they do act, it's simply too little too late," was the reply. "We have word of money and French soldiers to be shipped in at Moidart," Cluny went on, "but our men are starving and they're all are desperately worried for their kin. Terrible things are happening up north. You saw for yourself what they did to our wounded. Now they are rampaging through Inverness raping and murdering. Even the bairns are not safe. Hardly an hour passes but someone arrives with news of some new atrocity."

Old Cluny paused. All to clearly he could see what was to become of his own home and his own folk. Many a woman and child would pay a terrible price for the ambition and arrogance of the twenty-five year old Prince. Grief, anger and disillusionment clouded the chieftain's brow.

"I've left my cousin Davie a few miles down the strath," said Hamish. "He was caught by grape-shot in both legs. I managed to get him off the moor but we'll have to find somewhere for him to lie up or the dragoons'll have him for sure."

"We've two more really badly hurt casualties here," replied the chief. "I am having them moved to Creag nan Uamh. We'll leave enough provisions for a few weeks and old Rory to look after them. He has no family of his own and is willing to do what he can for them. You go, get Davie and meet up with them there. Young Ken can go with you to lend a hand with Davie but mind, I need both of you back as soon as possible."

Hamish knew Creag nan Uamh, a craggy mountain away to the west, deep in the Monadhliaths, the vast range of grey hills stretching from Speyside to distant Lochaber. He was also one of the very few who knew of the McPhersons' secret cave high up in the crags. He approved Cluny's choice for a field-hospital. Even if the Government forces did penetrate into those deserted wastes, the chances of them stumbling on the cave itself were virtually nil.

"Right, with your permission we'll leave at once," he said. "Do we return here or to the castle?"

"Better head straight to Ben Alder," was the reply. "By the time you get the three injured safely there and settled, Cumberland's rogues will no doubt be upon us here. They'll burn my castle, for sure. I'll pull back to the south and set up camp at the Ben Alder cage."

Hamish then headed for the fire where several clansmen were industriously baking salmon and roasting a deer. He could not remember when he had last had a cooked meal and he was ravenous. The fish and venison were washed down with some tolerably good ale that he was told was spoils of war, having been captured along with barracks.

Chapter 4

Having eaten his full, Hamish sliced some of the more tender bits of venison and wrapped them up to take along with a flask of brandy for Davie. The French were not much help in battle, he thought, but they do know how to make brandy. He hunted around the make-shift camp until he found Ken. Ken was another kinsman. Nothing remarkable about that as all the clan were in some way or other related to everyone else. Ken was a second or third cousin. He could not remember exactly and it did not matter. They all owed allegiance to Ewan McPherson of Cluny and therefore loyalty to one another. Ken was both small and young. At thirteen, he had been too young to march with the Jacobites on the long journey south when they penetrated into England as far south as Derby. Nor, therefore, had he been one of the dispirited army that withdrew from there through Carlisle and Glasgow, through Falkirk and Blair Atholl, to Inverness and to Culloden. For all that he was barely five feet, he was a plucky kid and Hamish was glad of his company and help.

The two forded the Spey again and struck up northwards towards Aviemore. At Alvie, they swung up on to higher ground. Not a moment too soon, it emerged, for they were only fifty yards off the track when they heard the sound of drumming hooves and the clink of the horses' bridles.

Shrinking into a copse of stunted birch trees, the pair froze, lying prone on the blaeberry plants that blanketed the ground beneath the trees. As they watched, a troop of about seventy cavalrymen passed below them.

As soon as the immediate danger had passed, Ken whispered "Shouldn't we try to warn Cluny?"

"There's nothing we can do," muttered Hamish, "We can't overtake that troop without being seen and then we could not outrun them. Cluny will have pickets placed and no doubt will get plenty of warning. He may even be able to set up an ambush. If our folk have enough guns and ammunition, those red coats will make brilliant targets. No! We have our orders and we stick to them."

Hamish and Ken lay silently in undergrowth for a full five minutes after the last sound of horses and men had died away. Then, with great caution, they rose and slipped noiselessly deeper into the scrub. An hour or so later they came to the place where Davie lay concealed. Hamish was surprised and secretly pleased that he found it difficult to locate. He had done his best to hide the injured man but was pleasantly taken aback at just how effective the camouflaging was. However, Davie was not well. He was in a fever and sweat was pouring from him. The blood had seeped through the dressings on his legs but was now crusted. The feet below the level of the bandages were red and inflamed.

Hamish tried to encourage his friend to eat, but the poor fellow was barely conscious. Hamish poured a trickle of brandy into Davie's mouth, but most of it ran out again. With some difficulty the patient was helped on to Hamish's broad shoulders and the three of them set off westwards, climbing slowly and steadily, leaving Strathspey far behind them. The day was wearing on when at last they passed through a high col and could see the dark, craggy mass of Creag nan Uamh ahead. For the last two miles or so they took special care. It would be all up for them if English soldiers spotted them at any point in their journey, but how much worse if they inadvertently led the avenging soldiers to the refuge of the other wounded highlanders!

Ken scouted ahead and bit by bit they inched their way up under cover of the deep heather and the birch scrub to the foot of the scree slope. There Hamish called a halt. It was already dusk and the three waited a full hour until the night shadows had all but closed around them before making their final, silent approach.

The mouth of the cave was at the top of the scree slope, the latter the product of erosion of the cliff that towered above. A rock-fall in the mists of time had deposited a boulder the size of a small house right in front of the cave. Indeed, this boulder sagged back against the face and, from even a matter of yards, looked part of the face itself. Even a quite observant man could pass along the foot of the scree slope a thousand times and never guess the presence of a cave. Its existence was a closely-guarded McPherson secret and it had played a vital part several times in the turbulent history of the clan. Reaching the cave was, in the event, something of an anticlimax. Rory and his party had not arrived. Hamish and Ken gently laid down the now nearly delirious Davie deep inside the cave, feeling their way into the blackness. After making the sufferer as comfortable as possible on a rough bed of heather, Hamish set about lighting a fire. The cave was spacious enough for them not to be choked and the sheltering boulder at the mouth ensured that no light would escape to betray their presence.

Chapter 5

Ken mounted watch, sitting in the shelter of the protective
boulder in a position where he could hear, if not see, anyone
approach in the gathering darkness. After about forty
minutes, he heard the sound of a pebble trickling down the
scree, then silence. It may only have been a mountain hare
but the lad was keyed up, peering into the darkness and
straining his ears. Then he heard another movement, nearer
this time. Someone was approaching with evident caution.
He clutched his dirk and waited. Out of the shadows emerged
the hunched figure of a man. Old Rory! Even in the virtual
blackness, Ken recognised him. The old man wheezed his
way up the final few feet of the scree. He was obviously all
but totally exhausted. Silently the two, the old man and the
lad, exchanged a hand-shake.

"Thought I'd better spy out the place," gasped Rory, "It
would have been terrible if I'd led those lads back there into
an ambush. I left the others hidden in a peat-hag about half a
mile back and came on alone to make sure all was well. I
can't tell you how glad I am to see you!"

"And we you!" said Ken warmly. "Let's get Hamish and
we'll help you bring the wounded up the slope."

Leaving the now comatose Davie in the cave, the three hurried down to where the concealed men lay. Cluny had sent four strapping clansmen to help Rory carry the two injured men and supplies of dried meat and fish, together with a sack of oatmeal. Quickly and quietly, the enlarged party clambered back to the cave. As the men huddled round the fire and were now feeling better for having fed, they recounted the day's adventures.

"We were only a little behind you in leaving Ruthven," said Rory. "We forded the Spey just up stream of where the Tolmie joins it. Then one of Cluny's sentries came dashing down the track from the north. He shouted a warning of approaching soldiers and then plunged off across the river to raise the alarm. We were just starting to gain height when we heard thon dragoons galloping towards us. There's not much cover there at all but I remembered the old earth-house just uphill of the track. We barely reached safety there before the horses rode by.

"I waited a minute or two and then eased myself out. The horsemen had started to cross the river but, as you know, it's awful boggy there and if you don't know the crossing points you can get in a right mess. Well, they were struggling with water and mire up to their stirrups when our lads opened fire. Talk about sitting ducks! One by one they fell, some dead, some choking and spluttering in the bog or the river. Those the guns didn't get, the Spey surely will! Only a handful made it back to firm ground and the last I saw they were racing off northward.

"Aye, but they will be back, and back in force no doubt. I don't think Cluny will try a pitched battle, however. After Culloden, I think they're in no mind to make a stand. They'll just melt away into the night and leave Cumberland and his butchers to find an empty Strath.

"Anyway, we couldn't afford to linger, so we set off up the Gynack and Alit Mor as fast as we possibly could. I reckon that if anyone saw the direction we were heading they would think we were going to the Coignafearn Forest and would never guess that we would double back and pick up the track for here. I'm sure we weren't followed, so we should be safe enough here at least for a while."

That night they slept like dead men, the events of the last few days having utterly drained them. The next morning Hamish, Ken and the four clansmen set off back to rejoin their chief. It was with a heavy heart that Hamish left his cousin. He knew that Rory would do all that any man could for all three sick men, but Davie looked so far gone that Hamish doubted if he could possibly pull through.

Chapter 6

The march back was undertaken with the greatest care. The maximum use was made of every bit of natural cover. At times progress was painfully slow. Where they could not see far ahead, the group would hide in the heather until one had crawled forward to make sure the way was clear. This caution was vindicated. Twice extensive detours had to be made to put a safe distance between the fugitives and bands of Government troops. It became clear that reaching Ben Alder and the McPherson hideout there before nightfall was out of the question. Although it was not raining, it was heavily overcast and a raw north-east wind was blowing. Two things were obvious. They must find shelter and, tonight, there could be no question of lighting a fire.

Ahead, and to the south, lay the dark, sparsely wooded mass of Creag Ruadh, rising over 1000 feet above the valley floor and the new military road from the south to distant Fort Augustus. Hidden at the east end of the Black Craig was Dun na Lamb, an ancient hill-fort whose origins were lost in the mists of time. It had had no military significance for centuries and there was little risk of its existence being known to any who were not natives of the surrounding glens. Hamish decided this was the best option for the night. In the deepening shadows of evening, the highlanders crossed the military road and melted into the juniper and birch scrub that lined both sides of the headwaters of the Spey. The ascent of the Black Craig was made in near total darkness. Dun na Lamb is a natural strong-point, reasonably accessible from the west but secure on the other three sides because of crags that, whilst just climbable in daylight, were virtually impossible to scale in the dark.

Hamish went on ahead, inching his way through the scrub and then over the heavily eroded earthen wall on the north-west corner of the stronghold. Still moving with the utmost caution, he established that the place was deserted. He returned to his companions and soon they were settled reasonably comfortably in the lee of one of the ancient walls. From the northern parapet of the enclosure they could look down into the blackness of the glen below, a blackness broken here and there by the twinkling lights of camp-fires, for the military road from Loch Ness and the Great Glen, having crossed the Corrieyairack Pass, traversed the valley below. The men took turns at sentry duty and the night passed uneventfully.

As the first signs of dawn lit the sky in the north east, the highlanders slipped noiselessly out of Dun na Lamb. They made their way across the swampy ground of Strath Mashie, up by Linn of Pattick, until, skirting the forbidding heights of Aonach Beag, they reached Ben Alder. Hamish knew that long before they set a foot on the Ben, their presence would be noted and runners would be carrying news of their approach to Cluny. For all that, he heard and saw nothing. The hillside seemed totally devoid of life or movement. Just when they started to swing east towards Loch Ericht whose dark waters they had occasionally glimpsed far below, their path was suddenly barred by a dozen or more of as fiercesome a group of clansmen as had ever haunted a Redcoat's nightmares. Among them were several well-known faces and the enlarged group descended to where Cluny had set up his temporary headquarters.

Cluny's welcome was warm but curt.

"You got them there safe? Good! They'll be all right there as long as they stay out of sight. But come! We've work to do. I've word of French ships bringing supplies in at Moidart. We leave at dawn tomorrow and will need all the men we can muster to bring the cargo ashore before the English navy get word of the ships. You lads feed now and get some rest, for you may get neither food nor sleep for a week or more."

Chapter 7

So it was that, in drizzling rain and light mist, a band of some forty, with Cluny himself at the head, set off westwards at first light. The first twenty miles or so were covered at high speed. The highlanders were on familiar ground and kept to the upper slopes and high passes, a thousand feet and more above the valleys ten miles or so to the north where the Government troops were even at that moment searching and burning every last wretched cottage and byre.

They passed Corrour and the remote Loch Treig, keeping going westwards until they reached the head of Glen Nevis where they swung north up the high col to the east of Aonach More. Here, the pace changed abruptly. A scout crawled a couple of hundred yards ahead of the main party, only signalling for them to follow when he was sure the way was clear. Other look-outs took up positions to the east and the west, keeping their eyes peeled for Redcoats. So, at a snail's pace, they descended unobserved into the shelter and relative safety of Leanachen Forest. They rested beside a burn, Cluny having posted pickets at various points around them. Towards dusk, the rain swept in from the west in heavy squalls, a source of increased discomfort, but with the blessing that it provided cover for the tricky crossing of the valley of the Spean and the swollen waters of the river itself.

At Gairlochy, at the south end of Loch Lochy, the tired and sodden men met up with several of Cameron of Lochiel's men. Ewan Cameron of Lochiel was a cousin of Ewan McPherson of Cluny. Both, in the Highland fashion, were more commonly called by the name of their lands, Lochiel and Cluny, respectively. Lochiel's clansmen had set up a crude camp near where the River Arkaig poured its peaty waters into Loch Lochy. They had an elaborate system of lookouts and signalling so they were safe enough to have a fire. Soon the wet and hungry McPhersons were drying out their sodden plaids and were eating trout and venison.

Having fed, the men exchanged news. None of it was good. Those who had escaped the bloody scenes of Culloden had tales of massacre, not just of those in arms, but of helpless women and children. It was now over a week since the battle and the word was that Cumberland's forces were preparing for a summer of burning and slaughter. Lochiel and his Camerons, together with the Macdonalds, had thought that those loyal to the Prince could re-group in Lochaber, but they were so few that even the most fanatical agreed it was futile to continue the struggle. The French were bringing supplies and gold, but no army. All too clearly the cause was lost and it would soon be time for each man to look after his own as best he could.

Cluny, Coll Macdonald, Lochiel and one or two other clan leaders held a council of war. The French frigates were due any day and it was generally agreed that it would not be in the Prince's interest for the captains of the French vessels to learn the full extent of the tragedy at Culloden at this stage.

At dawn the next morning, a force of over one hundred highlanders, principally Camerons and McPhersons, set off westwards along Loch Arkaig. Cluny, Macdonald and

Lochiel went by boat, four of Lochiel's men pulling on the oars. The boat was left at the western end of the Loch and the whole party pressed on due west until Loch Morar came into view. Then they swung south, gaining height rapidly to take up a commanding view over the Sound of Arisaig. The mid-afternoon visibility was excellent, but not a sign of mast or sails could be seen. Hiding any disappointment or frustration, Lochiel despatched sentries to take up key positions at various vantage points overlooking the sea and also at the eastern approach from Glenfinnan to guard against a surprise attack on land by Government troops.

Chapter 8

There was nothing to be done but wait, a nerve-racking time that dragged on all through the next day. At nightfall nothing had changed, but the following morning, two sets of masts hove into view. A low sea mist blanketed the Sound and all that the watchers on the hillside could see were the bare top-masts of two ships piercing the fog and creeping painfully slowly towards land. What they could not see were the ships' boats that were hidden in the mist and which, each with eight sailors at the oars, were towing the frigates toward the shore. A look-out on the top-mast of each ship shouted directions and this was the only sound disturbing the morning peace. A couple of hundred yards or so off-shore, the ships dropped anchor. Cameron and Cluny, each with several of their clansmen, hurried to the beach. The ships were invisible but, across the open water, the noise of orders shouted in French, the rattle of anchor chains and the general hubbub of the ships being made ready to off-load their cargo could be clearly heard.

Cameron fired a pistol, counted to five, fired a second, counted to five and, at his nod, one of his men fired a third. He counted to ten, nodded, and a final shot was fired. Through the mist came answering shots. The agreed recognition signals had been exchanged. Then followed a strange silence, eventually broken by the creaking of oars. Through the mist loomed one of the ship's boats. From it leapt an impressively dressed French officer.

Cameron seized him by the hand.

"We were starting to get worried about you," he said. "The English navy have been seen nosing in and out of the sea lochs and I was worried that you might have fallen foul of them."

"We very nearly did," replied the Frenchman. "They spotted us off the south of Eigg the day before yesterday. We turned south and were able to keep ahead of them. We soon realised we could not out-run them, although we did keep them out of cannon-range. As soon as it was dark, we turned east, assuming they would expect us to make for the open sea to the west. However, at dawn, there they were only five miles south-west of us. The wind had fallen right away and for most of the morning all we could do was to look at each other. At one point they lowered their boats and it looked as if they were going to try to tow the ship into gun-range. However, they obviously thought better of it, which is a pity because we could have blown their boats clean out of the water before they could bring a gun to bear!

"Then, in early afternoon a slight breeze from the south-west got up. We hoisted everything we had and sailed northwards. We sorely wanted to stand and fight, there being two of us and only one of them, but the captain did not want to risk the cargo, so we tacked off to the north west. It is just as well we did not make a stand because our look-outs spotted sails to the west. We knew there were only our two French ships in the vicinity so we had to assume it was the enemy. We changed tack and, for the rest of the day, we ran north before the wind. At night-fall we were nearly at Skye, so we took a north-west heading. The English at this point were some seven miles behind us.

"As soon as we lost sight of them in the dark, we steered slightly south of west for perhaps half an hour and then hove to. It was a risk to take, but it paid off. They were so close we could hear their voices getting louder through the darkness and then fading away. We stood by our guns all night and, at dawn, there was no sign of them. The wind had shifted to the west, so we made good time until we passed the Arisaig peninsular. Then it fell away and we met this infernal mist. There was nothing for it but to lower the long-boats and haul the ships in."

"Well, you're here now, and my scouts on the Arisaig point will give early warning if the English discover you slipped past them in the night. I suggest we unload with all speed."

"But of course," said the Frenchman. "The guns and ammunition were loaded first, being the heaviest. On top of them are the food and liquor supplies. We'll unload them first. We also have the special cargo which is in six casks in the captain's own quarters. I think you and I had better supervise the unloading of them."

With that, he shouted various orders and French and Scot, side by side, set to with a will. The brandy and wine casks and the sacks of wheat were loaded into the long-boats, there being much shouting and general confusion because, although the mist was lifting, the ships were still invisible from the shore. Cameron and Cluny were rowed out to the larger of the French vessels. As they passed under the stern of the smaller one that was lying slightly closer to shore they could read the name "Mars" on the stern. The second ship was the "Bellona".

The "Bellona's" captain had organised a small detail of men on the poop-deck and soon, one by one, small, but extremely heavy, casks were lowered into the boat. Without waiting for more cargo, the oarsmen pulled for the unseen shore. When they made a landing, Cluny roared for Hamish and another five of his men.

"Get these up to the tide-line," he said, "and guard them with your lives."

The six men struggled up the beach, each man-handling a heavy cask. They put them down and stood in an out-ward facing circle round them. They had not been told what the casks contained, but it was not difficult to guess.

Chapter 9

Nearly an hour elapsed and the mist was lifting rapidly in the morning sun. The outline of the French frigates could now be clearly seen through the mist. Suddenly there was the report of two flintlocks being fired from far out on the peninsular.

"The English ships must have been sighted," shouted Lochiel.

Near panic ensued. The last of the long-boat's cargo was flung, rather than unloaded, on the shore. Highlanders grabbed the supplies that were piled on the beach and hurried them into concealment. The two French captains were yelling orders and already there was the noise of anchors being weighed. The wind was minimal, scarcely causing a ripple on the loch, but the French were naturally very anxious not to caught on a lee shore with an enemy to windward, even in the lightest breeze. The long boats positioned themselves under the bows of their mother-craft, cables were slung and soon the oarsmen were rhythmically pulling and the ships almost imperceptibly were heading to open water.

Hamish stood at his post, waiting for further orders. He looked out over the loch. Loch na Uamh, 'the loch of the cave'. His mind went to Creag na Uamh, 'the mountain of the cave', and he wondered how his kinsman Davie was faring. It seemed an age since he had left him in the care of Rory. Hamish thought gloomy thoughts about the chances of recovery for one so badly injured.

The crackle of gun-fire from the east broke in on his thoughts. Cluny and Cameron of Lochiel raced along the shore toward them.

"It's that rascal, Macdonald of Boisedale," gasped Cluny. "He's got a small army with him and I'm sure its not to help the Prince. Lochiel's men fired a few shots to make them keep their heads down but you had better get moving with that lot. We'll hold them off for a bit and then parley with them. Head for Glen Pean. We should make better time than you and overtake you before you get there."

Lochiel detailed six of his men and the twelve, under the command of Lochiel's brother Archibald, were soon out of sight, heading up into the mountains. Behind them the remaining forces of Cluny and Lochiel formed a defensive position round the pile of stores. If it came to a fight, it would be a very unequal one and the two leaders were gloomy about the possible outcome. From far out at sea came the boom of naval cannon and then, from much closer, the sound of the French guns in reply. The noise re-echoed around the surrounding hills like a continuous peal of thunder. "That should help that rogue Macdonald realise who the real enemy is," muttered Lochiel as he grasped his pistols.

Out in the loch, the French vessels were nearing the more open waters of the Sound of Arisaig. The sun, climbing higher in the sky, was rapidly burning off the remaining mist and the light breeze was steadily freshening. As the visibility improved, the ghostly shapes of, first one, then two British war-ships could be discerned through the haze. Even before they were in range, the nearer of the two opened fire with its bow-chaser. The shot fell some three hundred yards short, throwing a great spout of water into the air. Both the French frigates were, by this time, cramming on every available stitch of canvas. This, however, made little difference to their speed, so without difficulty they were able to recover their long-boats and their crews.

A slow motion chase began, with the British sloops firing periodic ranging shots. These at first fell short, but the tell-tale splashes were creeping ever closer to the withdrawing French ships. Meanwhile, the French stern-chaser cannon opened fire. These had slightly more range, but, when the cannon balls did score a hit, it was at the extreme limit of the guns' range and no great damage ensued. The breeze was definitely strengthening as the craft pulled further and further from the land. The gap had closed and both sides were now scoring hits, still with little serious effect. Then, in a surprise manoeuvre, both French frigates swung to starboard. The gap between the opposing sides closed dramatically. The French fired a broadside at the approaching English. Many shots missed their targets but sufficient accurate shots struck home to leave gaping holes in the sails. The British ships slewed round and started to bombard with one salvo after another. However, the damage to sails and rigging cut their speed and, as the French frigates again turned their sterns to the wind, the British sloops rapidly fell astern. The stern-chasers on the French vessels kept up a steady barrage, whilst British broadsides thundered in reply. Eventually, as both sides' shots were increasingly falling short of their targets, the guns fell silent and the British sloops heeled round to head northwards.

Chapter 10

Whilst all this was going on, there had been developments on the shore. The clan chief, Macdonald of Boisedale, had sent forward one of his men with a white flag. Reluctantly, and only because they were greatly outnumbered, Lochiel and Cluny agreed to parley. Macdonald himself, flanked by four hefty clansmen, came up to the circle of men guarding the recently unloaded supplies.

"What business have you here?" demanded Lochiel. "This is the property of your Prince and I demand safe conduct to Arkaig."

"Aye, and much good it will do the Prince," said Macdonald with a sneer. "Where is he now? I hear he ran for his life at Culloden. No doubt he has saved his precious skin, but without a thought as to what will happen to the highlands now. Meanwhile, my people face starvation. Some of those supplies would make all the difference and I reckon the Prince has as much a duty to his people as his people have to him."

Lochiel could not help feeling that Macdonald, rogue though he was, had something of a case.

"I will not bandy words with you," he replied, however. "My duty is plain. I hold this stuff for Prince Charles and you must let us through."

"I don't want bloodshed, but either you give us a fair share or you have a fight on your hands. You take half and we'll take half. I'll give you a receipt for you to pass on to your precious Prince, if you ever see him this side of Paris. Be sensible. The battle has been fought and lost. It's every man for himself and his kin now. These are spoils of war! Let's divide them equally and part as friends."

There was a certain compelling logic to this, but Lochiel was determined to stand firm. However, just as he was about to speak a cannon roared out in the Sound and a ranging shot threw up a great spout of water only a couple of hundred yards from where they stood. Any further argument was obviously pointless. Both Lochiel and Macdonald shouted orders and clansmen from both sides swooped down on the remaining casks and sacks. Cluny stumbled up the sands, weighed down by a huge sack of flour. The guns out at sea fired again and he glanced round in time to see several Highlanders drop, three obviously dead, whilst others were writhing in the sand, caught by deadly grapeshot. Friendly hands seized the fallen men and they were dragged to the relative safety of the dunes. A small pile of supplies still lay where they had been unloaded but no one would now risk crossing the exposed stretch of sand with the British sloops closing in fast.

Taking advantage of the natural cover provided by the Borrowdale burn, Cluny and Lochiel urged their men up the hillside. Macdonald's force, retreating to the east, lacked the advantage of natural cover and suffered several casualties as they withdrew. The sloops were now in shallow waters and, dropping anchor, launched long-boats crammed with heavily armed marines. For all their haste, however, the disembarking took time and they landed on an abandoned beach with only a few casks, sacks and corpses to show that the clansmen had ever been there. By this time both highland forces had put a mile or more between themselves and their pursuers. Knowing that these hill-men would outstrip his marines in a chase across the mountain, the British commander reluctantly but wisely called off any further pursuit.

High above the loch, Cluny gave his men a short rest. Far to the south, the French ships' masts could just be seen, crossing the distant horizon. The British warships lay at anchor in the bay. Of Macdonald's men there was no sign. Two minutes more, and the highlanders moved on, each man carrying a heavy cask or a sack, but still able to cover the ground at a steady six or seven miles an hour. They skirted round Loch Morar, maintaining their height until they reached the col that led to Glen Pean. Here, they caught up with Hamish and his party, struggling as these were with the heavy casks. Together, the re-united force pressed on to Loch Arkaig. The special casks were carefully loaded on the waiting boat and Cluny, Lochiel and his brother set off by water for Achnacarry at the east end of the loch. The others followed on foot. Even these hardened Highlanders, used as they were to traversing vast distances on foot, were feeling the strain and it was a very tired and hungry party that arrived it the Achnacarry camp late in the evening. Lochiel had anticipated this and hot food and French brandy was waiting for every man. All immediate danger was past. Pickets were posted at every strategic point and the weary clansmen gratefully settled down to sleep.

Chapter 11

The whole of the day following was spent in frantic activity. Anticipating the inevitable arrival of the Redcoats, Lochiel had ordered the evacuation of all non-combatants. The women and children were sent to the high shielings above Glen Mallie. Shielings were crudely built shelters that the herdsmen lived in during the summer months when they took their black cattle up to the high hanging valleys for the summer pasture. In the short term, these would provide a safe haven. However, within three or four months, as the autumn gave way to winter, the refugees would have to descend once more to the more hospitable glens. This was a problem for the future, though, and the more vulnerable members of the clan would be safer in the sheilings than anywhere else for the time being.

At the same time, everything of value was being stripped out of all the houses. At regular intervals, those on picket duty reported and twice during the day runners arrived with news, one from northwards up the Great Glen and the other from Inverlochy, to the south. The news was all grim. In the aftermath of battle, the Redcoats had been turned loose to rape, pillage and murder as they saw fit. No highlander was exempt. Many who had not joined the rising at all and felt safe from Government vengeance stayed where they were and perished in the blazing ruins of their homes. Nor were the elderly or the very young spared. Lochiel and Cluny listened with increasing horror and frustration to the catalogue of atrocities. All hope of a successful resistance was clearly over and the only thing to do was to try to preserve their clans from the marauders for as long as possible. In due time, the uncontrolled wave of killing might be curbed.

The clan leaders spent most of the afternoon conferring. By evening they had decided to disperse, each taking his own clansmen back to whatever part of their own territory they thought might be safe. In the late evening, as the sun was sinking in the north-west sky, Cluny, Lochiel and Lochiel's brother, Archibald, loaded five of the six special casks back on to the boat. They rowed off into the shadows of the deepening gloaming. Soon the darkness swallowed them up completely.

The first rays of dawn were lightening the sky in the north-east when the boat returned. With a parting nod to each other, the three men joined their respective clansmen to catch a few hours sleep.

Hamish awoke with the rising sun and had barely breakfasted when he was summoned by Cluny. The chief was sitting by the loch, scratching on a flat stone with his dirk.

"The word is that a large force of Redcoats have marched from Inverness and have camped at the ruined fort at the south end of Loch Ness, the place they call Fort Augustus. There are already several hundred of them and it may be only a day or so before they are here in even greater strength. We can harry them, but we cannot hold them. I am heading for Lochaber but I want you to return to Ben Alder as quickly as you can.

"You are to take yon sixth cask and guard it with your life. I'll send seven good men with you. You are to stay out of sight and take no risks. You can take as long as you need, but at all costs get that cask safely to Alder. I'll meet you there when my business in Lochaber is finished.

"Your biggest problem will be crossing the Great Glen. The Redcoat scum are crawling all over it. They have boats on Loch Lochy and Loch Ness so any ideas of crossing by water are out. You have a choice of four short stretches of land, the longest, between Loch Linnhe and Loch Lochy being no more than nine miles. Lochiel's scouts say that sentries are posted at regular intervals on each. You won't find it easy, but you are a man I trust and I'm sure you will win through."

Hamish was temporarily lost for words. No one had said what the cask contained, but, what with the weight and with the care with which it was guarded, no one could doubt the value of the contents. And he was being entrusted with it!

"I'll try the marshy ground between Loch Lochy and Inverlochy. That's the nearest and we might just get through before the reinforcements from Inverness reach the southern end of the Great Glen. We'll go over the hill to Glen Loy this afternoon and wait for dusk at some vantage point from which we can see the position of the sentries. Then, after sunset, we'll try to cross."

"Good man," said Cluny warmly. "If anyone can do it, you can! I've seen you stalk stags and, if you can get within fifty feet of a red deer without being noticed, you'll pass a Redcoat five feet away and he'll never know you've been there! Now, take this stone. If you get tidings that Lochiel and I've been killed or taken, you get this to my Lord Lovat. Only to him, mind. No one else. It's the key to where the other casks are. Only he'll know how to read it. Now get your men together. Take Alan and Lachlan. They both know these lands like the backs of their hands. Then there's Gregor and Jamie. Non too bright, mark you, but you can trust them with your life and they're strong enough to trot all day long carrying that cask. Aye, and take Alistair, Dougie and Colin. Great lads, all of them, if it comes to sword-play. But watch thon Alistair! He's a hot-headed one, that one, aye spoiling for a fight. But a bra lad for all that! Now go! And we'll meet at Ben Alder."

Chapter 12

Hamish gathered his little band. They packed supplies that would see them through several days, indeed, all the way to Ben Alder if all went well. Then they headed up Glen Mallie at a fast pace. All were young and fit. Keeping up a steady five miles an hour even uphill was no problem. At mid-afternoon they crossed the ridge to a point that gave them a panoramic view down Glen Loy to the Great Glen to the east. From here on they moved with great caution, taking pains never to be silhouetted against the sky-line. Eventually, in early evening Hamish called a halt. The eight men were in a shallow hollow screened by thick heather and the odd bush. From here they could see in the distance the red uniforms of the Government troops.

It was a warm and tranquil evening. The slowly setting sun cast a rosy glow on the rolling mountains beyond the Great Glen. To the west the light cloud formation was lit up to give a heart-stopping sunset. A deep sadness swept over Hamish as he thought of the sorrows that had come and were to come on this beautiful land. He wondered how his family were faring back in Speyside. His two younger sisters would be struggling to support his widowed mother. Farming in such poor soil was always very hard, but, without a man to do the heavy work, life must have been grim for the three women since he left home over a year ago. He thought too of Christine, the childhood friend he had nursed secret thoughts of one day marrying. What chance had these three young women of escaping the rampaging military in their campaign of rape and pillage? Tears welled in his eyes and he forced himself back to his own present situation. The shadows were deepening in the valley below and the watch-fires of the Redcoats twinkled in the gloaming. Hamish tried to memorise the position of each and to plan a route that would give the best chance of a safe passage.

Towards mid-night he gave the signal and, one by one, the highlanders slipped out of their hiding place and noiselessly descended the ridge. As the ground began to level out, they dropped to their knees and, with painful slowness, advanced on all fours. A wide circle of light spread out from each watch-fire and the sentries could be clearly seen in the glow. Although in these northern latitudes it is never totally dark in mid-summer, the gaps between the fires seemed pools of inky blackness. The ground on the floor of the valley was one continuous bog from which water slowly percolated into the River Lochy. The river itself was neither wide nor deep, but the clansmen knew that crossing it would be the most dangerous part of the whole endeavour. The stones underfoot would be slippery and they would have to leave the friendly shelter of the heather and scrubby bushes and become awfully exposed in mid-stream.

The line of watch-fires was on the relatively dry west bank of the river. The gaps between each were more or less uniform, although here and there boggy ground had induced the soldiers to leave a wider space. It was through one such gap that Hamish, by a gesture of his hand, directed his little band. Silently and with the utmost caution, they inched their way forward, with the bog water seeping into every stitch of

52

their clothing. As they neared the river bank, a furtive movement was heard a hundred yards or so upstream. The eight men froze. Again came the sound, someone slipping on a stone in mid-river. Then there was a shout from one of the soldiers on picket duty. A sentry ran along the bank with a blazing torch in his hand. Out in the river, three dimly lit figures were caught trying to cross. Other Redcoats came running. Four of them splashed through the bog only a couple of yards from Hamish. Fortunately their eyes were on the man with the torch and the scene in the river so they did not see what was near-by. Two soldiers stopped, raised their muskets and fired. One of the fugitives fell and the other two scrambled for cover on the far bank.

An officer shouted for more torches and a dozen Redcoats leapt into the river in pursuit. Hamish gave whispered instructions and the group began to worm their way back the way they came. Last to leave, Hamish glanced back across the river. The soldiers' torches flickered like fire-flies among the gorse and juniper scrub. Then, in the pool of darkness that was the river, he saw a movement. The man who had been shot was drifting down in the sluggish current and, though clearly injured, was not dead. Taking a terrible risk, Hamish slid as soundlessly as an otter over the bank and into the chill water. He scrambled rather than swam through the three-foot deep stream, seized the wounded man and dragged him to the bank. The other seven had by now covered a couple of hundred yards, carefully hauling the precious cask with them. More slowly, and with infinite caution, Hamish followed them. At last they reached the rising ground they had so recently descended and the cover of the undergrowth there. A farther two hundred yards and they stopped to re-group. Hamish caught up with them, stumbling under the weight of a very heavy and inert man.

In the distance, they could still see the flickering torches. The sound of shouts and of the occasional shot came to their ears. However, the pursuit was taking the soldiers away to the east so the immediate danger was past. They held a whispered council of war. Any thought of pressing forward over the river was abandoned. The wounded man must be borne to some safe hiding place where friendly hands would do what they could for him. If the fugitives who were being hunted down by the soldiers were not caught, the whole area would be alive with Redcoats from first light. The only sensible course was to withdraw as fast as possible back up Glen Loy and, if necessary, all the way back to Achnacarry to hand over the man who had been shot.

Taking turns, they carried the wounded man and the cask and trotted rapidly through the semi-darkness. Hamish decided to gamble that the hub-bub down in the valley would have aroused any Redcoat patrol that might have lain in their path and that he would have got ample warning of the soldiers' presence. The gamble paid off. By dawn they had reached the shelter of Lochiel Forest and Hamish judged it safe not only to take a rest but also to light a small fire deep in a densely wooded hollow. Only now could they examine the extent of the wounded man's injury. He had been bleeding profusely from a head wound but this had now dried up. Alan, who had some skill at medicine, peeled back the crude bandage he had applied in the darkness in an effort to stem the flow of blood. The bleeding started again, but only very slightly.

"He's a lucky lad," pronounced Alan. "The ball only grazed his skull, knocking him out but doing no lasting damage."

The man groaned but still did not regain consciousness. The others stripped off his sodden plaid and made him as comfortable as possible by the fire. The sun was shining brightly now and each highlander unwrapped his own plaid and stretched it out over the clumps of heather to dry.

Chapter 13

After a short rest, Hamish sent Dougie and Alan back the way they had come. The two covered about a mile, then separated so that they could act as pickets. Concealed in the long heather at strategic positions that gave a commanding view, they settled down to maintain a careful watch, knowing that their lives and those of their companions might well depend on their remaining fully alert.

Meanwhile, Hamish had despatched Alistair and Colin back towards Achnacarry to make contact with Cameron's men. This took much less time than he had expected, for the two friends came upon one of the Cameron Clan's high shielings. In a hanging valley with lush summer grass growing on both sides of the sluggish waters of a small burn and a lochan, a herd of black cattle was grazing. These were tended by two Cameron families who were living in the crude shelters known in the Highlands as shielings. Of a dry stone construction with roofs thatched with heather, the buildings were intended only for summer use. In the late spring, the few cattle that had been kept alive throughout the winter months were herded up from the glens far down the mountainside to feed and to calve here during the summer months. Thus the thrifty clansmen made the most of the high-level grazing in the fine weather and ensured that the grasslands in the glens were left intact to provide fodder in the late autumn and early winter. In happier times, whole families moved up to these shielings and something of a holiday atmosphere prevailed. This year was different, however. The youngest children still played by the burn without a care in the world, but not so the older ones and the adults. Among them the sense of foreboding was almost tangible. Daily, one of the fit young men would cover the twelve-mile round trip to Achnacarry for news and to see if the Clan Chief had any fresh orders for them. The news seemed to get worse with each succeeding day.

Quickly, Colin explained their errand. The Camerons were a little fearful and rather reluctantly agreed to take responsibility for the wounded man. Colin remained at the shieling while Alistair relayed this message to Hamish. Recalling the two who were on picket-duty, Hamish led his men down to the shieling. It was now early afternoon. Over a hurried lunch news was exchanged. None of it was good. The latest word was that the Government troops were reinforcing their camp at the southern end of Loch Ness. Simultaneously, they were rounding up the clans-folk in all the neighbouring glens. There were harrowing accounts of the men being shot or hanged without any pretence at a trial. The younger women and girls were raped and the older ones driven from their cottages. Their homes were then put to the torch. Meanwhile, the livestock was being herded into hastily improvised markets. Already drovers from the lowlands were buying them up at knock-down prices and herding them southwards to the distant cattle-marts at Crieff and Perth. Fear ruled throughout the Great Glen and all the surrounding countryside. Even if the indiscriminate slaughter ceased, the next winter would take a dreadful second cull, particularly of the very young and the very old. Even those who managed to find sufficient food might still succumb to the cold of a highland winter if they had no roof over their heads.

Hamish absorbed all this. Having seen the level of military activity in the Great Glen the night before, he decided that to attempt to cross to the south side the following night would be suicidal. Reluctantly, because the route across the Glen passing south of Loch Lochy and north of Loch Linnhe was by far the shortest, he decided that they would have to work their way northwards and then attempt the crossing either to the north or the south of the relatively small Loch Oich. For safety's sake he decided to make a long detour round Loch Arkaig, then north by Glen Kingie eventually reaching Loch Oich by way of Glen Garry. The final decision as to whether to the pass north or south of the Loch could wait until they reached the high ground overlooking it. Many miles were thus added to the distance they would have to march, but prudence seemed to dictate this course of action.

Shouldering the cask, the little band made their way westwards, staying high up the mountain ridge that bordered Loch Arkaig. Although they had been assured that the Redcoats had not yet penetrated so far west as this, they took advantage of every available bit of natural cover. At times, when the path in front was not clear, a couple of the clansmen would scout ahead of the main party. In the event, this caution proved unnecessary, for they reached the end of Loch Arkaig and crossed the col that would bring them to the head of Glen Kingie without encountering either friend or foe. They dropped into the glen, loosing height rapidly, which was just as well as evening was upon them and they were naturally anxious to find somewhere safe and comfortable to spend the night. They reached a lochan and the dilapidated remains of an abandoned shieling. Although roofless, its remaining walls would break the chill evening breeze, and, more importantly, would screen from any enquiring gaze the small peat fire they lit. The usual sentries were posted and arrangements made as to who would stand watch throughout the night. Then the men rolled themselves in their plaids and slept fitfully until dawn.

Chapter 14

As usual, Hamish was anxious to press on. Breakfast over, the men cautiously made their way down to Glen Garry. They were now leaving the lands of the Camerons and entering McDonnel territory. Passing through this, they would then be at the southern end of the lands of the Grants. Hamish was uncertain of how they might be received by the McDonnels. This clan had not too conspicuously supported the Jacobite cause, even when Prince Charles' star was in the ascendancy. Now they might either curry favour by capturing and handing the group over to the Government forces, or, more likely, would regard the cask and its contents as legitimate spoil. From the Grants, he knew he could expect no help. Their chief had clearly distanced himself from the Jacobite cause.

Moving forward with infinite caution, the clansmen sought the cover of the pines and birches that surrounded the River Kingie. Yard by yard, they made their way to where the Kingie joined the Garry. Here, concealed among the boulders and the scrub, Hamish called a halt. He sent Colin and Dougie ahead across the River Garry. The two crawled forwards for several hundred yards. Once they were satisfied the way ahead was clear, they eased their way back to the main party. Still exercising the greatest care, the men one by one forded the Garry and found shelter in the scrub on the far bank. At once they began to climb the steep northern slopes, working their way eastwards as they did. Far below they could see the smoke rising from the chimneys of the little clachan of Tomdoun, the houses themselves out of sight below the ridge. Keeping to just below the tree-line, the clansmen made their way eastwards towards Loch Oich and the Great Glen. It was a brilliantly sunny summer day, but, for once, Hamish wished for rain, mist or anything to impair the enemy's vision. The need for caution meant slow progress and all thoughts of crossing the Great Glen that night were out of the question. Lachlan, who knew this area better than the others, spoke up.

"There used to be a settlement at Loch Lundie but it was abandoned long ago. However, we can probably find reasonable shelter there for the night."

"How long is it since you were last here?" asked Hamish.

"Four or five years, I suppose," was the reply, "but I doubt if anything's changed in that time. We'd better take great care for all that. You never know where the Redcoats may show up next."

"You know the place," said Hamish. "You spy out the land while we wait here."

Lachlan eased his way up to a rocky outcrop from which he had a commanding view over the loch. What he saw appalled him. The settlement had obviously been re-inhabited. A small herd of cattle and a few sheep grazed by the loch and a lazy column of smoke coiled out of the hole in the roof that served as a chimney of the larger of two buildings. A couple of children were playing, whilst a man was swinging a sickle, cutting hay. That was not what shocked Lachlan. From his lofty vantage-point, he could see a detachment of ten or twelve Redcoats closing in on the settlement, these being totally concealed from the children and their family.

Lachlan backed off, writhing along the ground until he first felt safe to crawl and, eventually, to run. He quickly covered the ground and blurted out his report to Hamish.

"Come on now," said Alistair in hoarse and angry whisper. "We can't just sit here and do nothing. Let's ambush these devils before they reach the cottages."

Before Hamish could reply there came the sound of several shots from down in the valley below. Quickly, but very cautiously, the clansmen crept to the top of the ridge. Parting the heather, they looked down in horror. The two children lay quite still and, even at the long range, splashes of red on their little bodies were all too evident. The man with the sickle was writhing on the ground, struggling to rise and cursing his attackers. One of the Redcoats, a broad tall figure with a fiery red beard advanced on the wounded man, his sword in his hand. A click on his right hand side startled Hamish. Alistair was taking careful aim with his musket.

"Don't fire, you fool," said Hamish in a whisper. "You can't help and you'll get us all killed."

A furious Alistair turned towards him but, even as he opened his mouth to speak, a hideous cry reached their ears. The bearded soldier had skewered the prostrate man.

Meanwhile a terrified woman shot out of the nearer of the cottages. Taking in the scene at a glance, she ducked back in and slammed the door. The Redcoats closed in on the building. Hamish counted them. Eight, nine, ten, eleven, twelve. Although it was too great a range to see any insignia, the red-bearded man was clearly in charge. Three of the soldiers started to kick the door in turn. The eventual outcome was all too clear. Hamish signalled to the others to withdraw. Once over the ridge, the eight men huddled together for a whispered conference.

"We can't do much but we ought to do what we can," said Lachlan.

"The best we could hope to do is to get seven or eight of them before they get the last of us. I'm game to try if you are," said Dougie.

"No," said Hamish, "we're too late to help those poor folk and we have our own mission to complete."

"I can't just walk away from what we've seen. Think what that woman's going through even as we speak," replied Alistair. "I want that animal with the red beard. He's mine!"

"Our orders come first," said Hamish in an angry whisper. "We must get that cask through to Ben Alder."

"Let Alistair and me ambush them down the track back to Loch Garry," said Dougie. "They're bound to follow the burn down. If we head them off, we can create a diversion that will help the rest of you reach Loch Oich and even if we get killed we'll at least take some of them with us."

Hamish knew he had a potential mutiny on his hands and realised that Dougie was offering him a way out.

"All right," he whispered. "On you go! And the best of luck to both of you!"

Chapter 15

Alistair and Dougie moved swiftly back down the hill and were soon lost from sight. The remaining six eased their way back up the ridge. Three Redcoats were lounging around outside the cottage whose shattered door now lay flat on the threshold. Every two minutes or so another would emerge from the building, buckling his belt and grinning. The last man came out, bloodstained sword in hand. He walked over to one of the children and wiped the blade clean on the child's pathetic clothing. One of the men set fire to the thatch and within minutes the hovel was ablaze from end to end. Hamish felt angry tears burning his eyes. He knew only too well that this scene was being repeated over and over again all across his beloved Highlands. Meanwhile, the Redcoats started to file off down the path beside the burn. At a small rocky outcrop above the river it narrowed and they were forced into a straggling single file. Suddenly, a shape rose as if from nowhere behind the last man. A hand clamped the Redcoat's mouth shut whilst simultaneously a razor-sharp dirk slipped up under his ribs and into his heart. Even as his body was being lowered noiselessly to the ground, exactly the same thing happened to the soldier in front of him. It took Alistair and Dougie only seconds to strip the bodies of pistols and muskets. The two corpses entered the fast-flowing river with only a soft splash. Then the two clansmen melted into the shrubbery.

The absence of the two dead men passed unnoticed for several minutes. Indeed, it was only when the path crossed the river that the detachment closed up and waited rather uncertainly that they realised that they had lost two. Even as they stood by the ford, a flash of red upstream caught their eyes and, tumbling over one rock after another, came the corpses of their missing men. Horror marked each face. The red-bearded man issued orders. Unwillingly, the remaining men retraced their steps, their muskets at the ready. Tightly bunched together they carefully moved up the path, none of them willing to be at the front as they reached the part where the track narrowed. However, the soldiers spilled out the other side to find an empty field ahead of them. They took up defensive positions, every sense alert for the slightest rustle in the birches or the heather, but sound came there none. At length the leader turned to his men.

"The cowards are gone," he said. "There's nothing more we can do. We'll go back and report."

Gratefully the men turned back down the path. Rounding the corner of the rock outcrop, the first man nearly tripped over the prostrate form of a Redcoat. Only then did it dawn on them that only eight men had safely made the journey up the path. The other two's dirked bodies, stripped of weapons, lay where they had fallen.

The remaining eight were now thoroughly unnerved. It took all the red-bearded officer's authority to prevent the withdrawal becoming a headlong flight. Having achieved some semblance of military discipline, he led the demoralised men down the track. The first few hundred yards passed uneventfully. However, as the party crossed a clearing, two muskets rang out almost like one.

The officer dropped, clutching his chest. The man behind him fell, bleeding profusely from a terrible head wound. Before the remaining six recovered, a barrage of pistol and musket shots crashed from the surrounding thickets. Three more men fell. The other three hurriedly levelled their muskets and fired, then sought cover. An eerie silence followed, broken only by the groans of injured men. A stalemate followed, during which no one moved. Alistair hurriedly reloaded his musket. Then he called out in Gaelic to Dougie. Again he called, but the only result was a volley of musket fire from the concealed Redcoats. The musket balls whistled dangerously close, but harmlessly, through the birch branches above him.

Gingerly, he crawled backwards, abandoning as he did so, the guns he had taken from the slain soldiers. A slight movement in the heather on the far side of the clearing caught his eye. A tiny patch of red was just visible. Alistair eased his way round the trunk of a gnarled Scot's pine and carefully sighted along his remaining musket. He squeezed the trigger. The roar of the gun was followed by a cry of anguish. Without waiting a needless second, Alistair slipped back into the cover of the brushwood behind him. This was not a moment too soon, for two muskets crashed out a volley that was followed by the sharper crack of pistol-fire. The bullets slashed through the heather around the base of the tree he had just left. Knowing the soldiers would now lose precious seconds reloading, he hurried over to where he had last seen Dougie. Dougie was dead. A lucky shot had smashed the top of his skull to a messy pulp. There was nothing Alistair could do for his old friend and now discretion demanded he withdraw. Before doing so, however, he dragged the Dougie's body up the slope behind which it had fallen and placed it face down in a position where a keen pair of eyes on the other side of the clearing might just discern a scrap of clothing. Then he reloaded his own and Dougie's musket and waited. After several minutes the heather stirred on the far side. A wary face peered across. Alistair aimed and fired. This time there was no sound. The soldier ducked his head back, having suffered no more than a terrible fright. While the soldiers had their heads down, Alistair poked the now-empty musket through the heather in front of the body of the unfortunate Dougie. From a distance, it might look as if the dead man were sighting down the gun and this would encourage the Redcoats to keep under cover. Hoping this might win him a few precious minutes, Alistair hastily retreated. It was not the three remaining Redcoats he feared. Indeed, there might now be only two, depending how badly hurt the man he had winged was. The big risk was that the crackle of gun-fire re-echoing round the mountains would bring government reinforcements in overwhelming strength.

Chapter 16

From their vantage point on the crag high above the settlement, Hamish and his companions had watched the Redcoats form up and start the descent down the trail to the Great Glen far below. They stayed motionless for some ten minutes after the last soldier had passed out of sight. Then, very cautiously, they made their way eastwards, down the steep slope, past the still-burning cottage and up the ridge on the far side. They were more than half-way up the ascent when the first shots echoed up from the tree-lined track far below. What was happening there was hidden from their view. With a heightened sense of urgency they pressed on up the slope. As they reached the top of the ridge, they dropped to all fours so as not to be silhouetted against the sky-line. Bit by bit, they eased their way forward until they had a near bird's eye view of Loch Oich and, in the distance to the north, the ruins of Fort Augustus.

Fort Augustus was one of the forts built to enable the distant London government to control the often-turbulent Highlands. Originally built at the small hamlet of Kilchumein, the Fort had been rebuilt at the south end of Loch Ness by General Wade in 1730 and re-named after the nine-year son of King George, William Augustus, the Duke of Cumberland. Sixteen years later this very same Prince would win the epithet of

"Butcher" by his conduct at the battlefield of Culloden and his treatment of the Highland people in the months that followed. Lord Lovat had seized and destroyed the fort less than a year before. The ruins had not been repaired, but, even at the considerable distance between the silent watchers on the hillside and the ruins, serried ranks of military tents could be seen. Among the tents, the red uniforms of government soldiers were clearly visible. Horses were stabled among the ruined buildings of the Fort. Beyond the tents was a crude enclosure in which was herded a seething mass of cattle. The marauding militia had set up the largest cattle-mart the Highlands had ever seen.

The unseen watchers on the hill looked down in awe. The sheer scale of the military operations below was breath-taking. More worrying, however, was the sight of a detachment of cavalry cantering towards them, obviously responding to the noise of gun-fire in the hills above. There was little that Hamish and his friends could do. There was definitely no time to retrace their steps across the glen behind them. There was no way forward that would not bring them into the view of any alert soldier in the Great Glen below. North-east was the only option, even though this would lead them into the possibly-hostile Grant territory. Moving as fast as discretion would permit, they sought the cover of the deep heather and the peat hags of the flat high plateau. All too soon, they reached a point where to press on farther would leave them exposed to the view of the first dragoons to ride up to the head of the glen, for before them stretched a featureless expanse of several miles of open heath-land. All they could do was to huddle down in the heather and hope.

Suddenly they saw a kilted figure break out of the trees the far side of the valley they had left behind and below them.

"Alistair!" breathed Lachlan. "But where is Dougie?"

"He won't be far behind," muttered Alan.

Alistair was meanwhile running across the valley floor, past the startled cattle and the smouldering buildings, then up the slope to the west. He worked his way up alongside the small burn, using the alders and birches that lined it to conceal his progress from anyone watching from below. By now, his friends realised that Dougie wasn't coming, indeed that only his death would have led Alistair to leave him. A shout from below attracted their attention. The first horsemen were spilling out into the valley. One, with keener eyesight than his fellows, spotted the fleeing Alistair. He raised his musket and fired, a futile gesture as the fugitive was clearly out of range.

Alistair crossed the sky-line, making no attempt to conceal his passage. The dragoons spurred their horses forward. Then, to the amazement of Hamish and his companions, a second figure in highland garb loomed up on the horizon following in Alistair's foot-steps. Two minutes later, came a third, then, after a further delay, a fourth.

"The cunning old fox!" said Colin, "It's Alistair! He's boldly marching over the crest, then crawling back to re-emerge below the ridge and re-cross it."

Again and again a highlander crossed the ridge. The dragoons now were struggling up the lower slopes. Every so often, one would raise his musket and fire. The range was steadily lessening, but it would take a lucky shot to hit the rapidly moving figure high above.

"Let's hope he doesn't leave it too late," muttered Hamish. "He's drawing them away from us, but he will have to run as he's never run before if the troopers are not to ride him down."

However, even as he spoke, the man in the kilt appeared starkly outlined on the horizon. A musket roared, and the distant figure flung his arms in the air and dropped motionless.

"He's hit! But maybe he's only winged!" said Colin.

But all hope ended when the first horseman reached the prostrate form. Reining in his horse, the soldier looked down at the bleeding figure spread-eagled on the heather. He raised his pistol and fired, the point-blank shot pulverising the unfortunate Alistair's skull.

Scarcely pausing to give the body a second glance, the trooper waved his comrades on. One after the other, horse and rider crossed the ridge and the dragoons fanned out, trying to pick up the trail of the phantom band of clansmen to the west. When the last Redcoat had disappeared, Hamish rose cautiously from his hiding-place.

"Now, let's move!" he said. "We'll cross this bog and get over the far ridge as fast as possible. We must just hope that Alistair's bought us enough time. Once we are a few miles into Grant lands, we'll swing away to the west and head for Lovat's territory."

Chapter 17

At a fast trot, the six crossed the open ground, ever waiting for the shout or the gun-shot that would tell them that they had been spotted. However, neither came. Through the peat-hags they ran, pausing every few hundred yards to let a new bearer take over the heavy cask. Once over the ridge, Hamish allowed a short breather. He looked around. To the right, only a couple of hundred yards off, the ground fell away sharply. Although he could not see over the edge, he knew that below the steep hillside lay the Great Glen with its string of lochs and its military roads and camps. Ahead was an expanse of heath, of bogs and of peat-hags, broken only by the occasional dark-brown lochan. To the west lay similar territory for a couple of miles, then the ground gently sloped down to give way to more heath-land, but this interspersed with clumps of stunted pines and with lochans surrounded by lush green grass and windswept junipers. Hamish knew that, farther on yet, the hillside fell away more steeply into Glen Morriston. This was another glen that had been pillaged by the victorious army and was no doubt well garrisoned. However, it had to be crossed, so he urged his friends to their feet and they marched on.

It was now early evening, and it had been a long day. Hamish was determined to get close enough to Glen Morriston before night-fall to have time for an hour or twos' sleep before slipping across the valley during the brief hours of darkness. The men were not only tired. They were hungry. The food they had brought with them was nearly exhausted and the inhospitable high ground offered no chance of living off the land.

The pace slowed as the approach to the high ground immediately above the glen demanded more caution. The hillside was now thickly wooded, giving, on the one hand, ample cover, but on the other, bringing the risk of unexpectedly meeting up with Redcoats. As they came round a corner, Lachlan blundered into a frightened goat. In an instant, the creature lay at his feet, its throat cut.

"What are you going to do with that?" demanded Hamish. "I know we are hungry but we can't light a fire and we can't eat it raw."

Lachlan slipped down to his knees and hacked the limbs off the beast, without wasting time skinning it.

"We'll take it this with us and hope we can light a fire before it goes off," he replied.

The party moved on. A mile or so on they stopped. Through the dense barrier of trees ahead they could see down into the glen, its floor some 500 feet below. Half a mile upstream was the ruin of a burnt-out cottage and, nearby, a small encampment with a dozen or so infantrymen in evidence. Downstream there was no sign of life, but a thin column of smoke rising over a knoll about a mile away indicated that there was someone down there and, following the harrying of the glen, that could only be another enemy camp. By gesture, rather than by words, Hamish appointed two sentries and encouraged the others to seize what sleep they could. So the next five hours passed, with each getting rest and each taking his turn to stand guard.

An hour after mid-night, in near total darkness, Hamish led his party down the grassy slope to the river. Upstream, the Redcoats' watch-fire glowed like a beacon in the dark. From time to time, it blinked as the dark form of a sentry passed in front of it. One by one, the clansmen slipped into the water, crouching down and forming a human chain across the swiftly flowing stream. The last man passed the cask to the man nearest the bank, then hurried past him and the other four to take up position at the head of the line in time to receive the cask as it was handed along. By the time he had it in his grasp, the man he had originally given it to had stumbled out on the uneven river-bed and stood in front of him ready to receive it. The next man was already passing him. In this way, passing the cask in relays, they reached the far shore in a matter of a minute or so. Hamish breathed a sigh of relief. The most anxious moments had been when they were exposed in mid-stream. Now that was past.

Great care was still needed, however. There was the ever present fear of mobile units patrolling the track which ran parallel to the river some twenty feet or so above it. The men crouched in the undergrowth on the river bank, while Hamish crawled up to the track. Lying in the lee of a thick clump of heather, he listened, straining his ears for the slightest sound. All he could hear was the chatter of the water on the stones below. He rose to his knees, his eyes trying to penetrate the darkness. Nothing! Only the distant flicker of the watch-fire. With an almost inaudible whistle, he signalled to the others. One by one, they strung themselves out up the bank, then passed the cask from hand to hand. Noiselessly, they all crossed the track and climbed the steep bank above.

75

Barely fifty feet up, Hamish froze, signalling as he did so for total silence. He strained his ears. The sound of the water was now almost inaudible and, apart from that, the silence seemed complete. Just as they began to relax, the sound of a footfall from down the track reached their ears. Then they heard another. And another! A patrol was approaching. There was no cover and nowhere to run to. They were exposed on the thinly-clad heather slope. One by one they sank down and drew their plaids over them, taking care to hide their hands, legs and faces, lest the white parts of their bodies be seen in the poor light. The irregular shapes of the plaids, dyed as they were with dull greens, browns and greys, made an excellent camouflage. All that was needed was rock-steady nerves and absolute stillness and silence. The footsteps grew louder and louder. Then, at last, they started to recede. Not a man among the six moved a muscle. At last there was silence, broken a few minutes later by the exchange, first of pass-words, then of greetings, at the camp upstream.

Hamish whispered instructions. One at a time, the clansmen crawled up the slope, passing the precious cask from hand to hand. Progress was painfully slow. Only one man moved at a time in order to minimise noise. Twenty feet, fifty feet, one hundred feet. Slowly they advanced and the flicker of the fire in the glen below gradually slipped out of sight. At last, Hamish felt it safe to stand up. Still exercising the greatest caution, the sure-footed highlanders climbed, reaching at last the safety of the ancient Invermorriston Forest, with its aged pines and thigh-deep heather. As the first glimmer of light brightened the sky in the north-east, the six turned west-wards towards the even denser forests of Glen Affric. They marched for another hour and then, reckoning the risk of being spotted in the growing day-light was now too great, they settled down to sleep. The thick heather so completely covered them that a trooper would almost need to ride right over them before he would notice them. The rising sun brought a welcome warmth, but hunger was now an ever present reality for each man.

Chapter 18

Apart from the perpetual buzz of bees in the heather and the occasional cackle of a pheasant, the silence of the hills was unbroken. Early in the afternoon, this changed abruptly. The sound of shouts and shots reached their ears. Throwing off sleep, each man grabbed his weapons. Peering cautiously through the heather, six pairs of eyes scanned the landscape to the north from where the sounds came. They could see nothing at first, then a column of black smoke spiralled up into the cloudless sky.

"Another clachan destroyed," muttered Lachlan.

Even as he spoke, they saw several dragoons on horseback and a larger number of infantrymen come into view about a mile away. At first it seemed the advancing men were coming straight to the spot where the six lay concealed. However, after ten anxious minutes, the soldiers swung away to the east. They were, however, close enough for the clansmen to see that, along with the Redcoats, were several figures, men, women and children and a dozen or so cows and sheep. Highlanders and beasts alike were being driven off into captivity and an uncertain future. Once again, all the six could do was to watch and to try to contain their anger and frustration.

An hour passed and nothing disturbed the peace of the moorlands. Hamish sent Lachlan forward to spy out the land. Forty minutes later he returned.

"Two poor devils dead," he reported tersely. "The cottages are all but burnt out. There's nothing we can do."

"No," said Jamie, "but we could cook the meat! The Redcoats will not notice if the smoke continues to rise for an extra hour or so."

"Risky," replied Lachlan. "What if they decide to come back?"

"True, they might. But it's not likely, is it?" Jamie said.

"All right," said Hamish decisively. "We must eat, but we must also be careful. Lachlan! You take the meat and place it where it will roast gently and then come back here. Jamie! You take Alan and find a safe vantage point where you can get early warning if the troops return. Every so often Lachlan can slip in and turn the joints and we will just have to hope we are cooking a meal for ourselves and not for some Redcoats!"

So the sentries were posted and the remaining four settled down impatiently to wait in the heather about half a mile from the smouldering buildings. At last, after several earlier trips to inspect his improvised kitchen, Lachlan returned with the well-roasted mutton in a large cauldron he had recovered from the ruins. The sentries were recalled and, having put another mile between themselves and the shieling, the ravenous men settled down to their first cooked meal since leaving Loch Arkaig. They ate their fill and were still left with a reasonable amount to take with them for a cold meal the following day.

Having eaten, the six set off once more. This time they headed north towards Strathglass. However, they kept to the high ground and, in late afternoon settled down to sleep, in anticipation of another long night march. At dusk they set off again, with the advantage that they were high enough up to escape the ravages of the voracious midgies that bred in innumerable multitudes in the boggy strath below. It gave them some little satisfaction to think that these nearly invisible allies were even now making the lives of King George's men an utter misery. It also meant that down in distant Glen Urquhart the Redcoats would be huddled round smoky fires in an effort to escape the worst of these man-eating insects.

It was in the chilly early morning hours that the clansmen reached the Glen and began to cross it. By then, there was not a midgie in sight, but the Redcoats were still reluctant to patrol far from their watch-fires. Thus Glen Urquhart was traversed without incident. By dawn they were well up in the Boblainy forest. As the sun rose, they again settled down to rest during the hours of daylight. Boblainy was a barren place. What was not boggy was rocky. Yet somehow, out of this unpromising terrain, a veritable forest had indeed grown, a mixture of pines, alders, birches and juniper. For all that there was no sign of mankind ever having so much as visited this wilderness, there was ample wild-life. Grouse and pheasant abounded. More than once the clansmen startled a herd of deer. Round the small lochans nested eider ducks and other wading birds. It was tempting to shoot one or other of the targets that frequently presented themselves, but prudence demanded that they not take such a risk. Taking ducks' eggs was a different matter, though, and a nourishing

80

if not very appetising meal was had of raw eggs. So they fed and so they rested. One last night-march, and the Great Glen would again lie before them.

Hamish had decided to attempt the crossing close to Inverness itself. On the face of it, this was foolhardy, to say the least. It did perhaps have the merit that, just because it was so potentially hazardous, the Government soldiers might be more lax. The recent spell of dry weather would mean that the River Ness would be as low as possible, but it was still a formidable obstacle. A night crossing would be particularly dangerous. By daybreak, the six were flat on their bellies, high on Dochfour Hill, gazing down on the loch of the same name. Beyond it was the River Ness, and, beyond that, the distant town of Inverness. The clachan of Dochgarroch seemed deserted. Nothing stirred on their side of the loch and the river, but on the far side they could pick out the line of General Wade's new road from Inverness to Fort Augustus and Fort William. At intervals along the road were small groups of soldiers on picket duty. Early though it was, a company of perhaps fifty mounted men and twice as many foot soldiers could be seen marching southwards, sometimes in full view, spread out over about three hundred yards, sometimes concealed among the trees.

Another day was spent tensely lying in the heather. Even those not on sentry duty could not relax. The very nearness of the enemy could not be forgotten for a minute, as the noise of men and beasts on the move echoed up from the valley below. Dreary hour followed dreary hour. At last the sun slipped below the western horizon and darkness fell in the wooded valley below, a darkness punctuated by the line of twinkling watch-fires at regular intervals, from Inverness in the north to the dark mass of Loch Ness in the south. At midnight, the six moved noiselessly down the slope to reach the River Ness several hundred yards down-stream from Loch Dochfour. Progress was now at a snail's pace. Yard by yard, they approached the river, its deep waters flowing silently through the night. Under the cover of a clump of alders, the men formed up. Once again they formed a chain and the cask was passed from hand to hand. The current was not strong, but the water ran deep. In the middle, the highlanders found themselves chest-deep, struggling to keep their feet on the slippery bottom. The tension was nearly unbearable. Spread out across the river, the men were desperately vulnerable. After what seemed an eternity, the last man clambered up the far bank.

The danger was still not over. Behind them were the dark waters of the river. Ahead, only a mere two hundred yards away, ran the Wade road with its random patrols and regular pickets. Cautiously the clansmen reduced the distance to the road to twenty feet, then lay in the shelter of some birch-scrub. Hamish decided that the safest procedure would be to cross the road one at a time at five minute intervals. This would minimise the noise at any one time. More pessimistically, it might enable the others to escape if any one man was spotted. The fourth man across would carry the cask. Alan crossed first. As sinuously as a weasel he slid out of the undergrowth and vanished into the darkness beyond. An uneasy silence followed. Then it was Jamie's turn. He, too, melted into the black depths of the woodlands beyond.

Hamish patted Gregor on the back, the signal for him to move. Slowly and silently he rose, concealing his slim body behind a tree trunk. Up the road, he could see the pinkish glow of the nearest picket's fire. Down the road there was only blackness. He hesitated, some sixth sense telling him all was not well. However, the silence was unbroken, so, sinking to his knees, he crept to the ditch lining the road. Again he glanced towards the watch-fire glow. It flickered and in that instant he realised a patrol was approaching. He pressed himself down in the ditch, knowing it was already too late to withdraw. Whilst the human eye may not distinguish one object from another in bad light, it can be remarkably quick to discern movement. His only hope was to freeze and to trust that the soldiers, their night-vision impaired by their recent exposure to the fire-light, might miss him in the dark. The sound of marching feet became louder, as did the murmur of voices. Gregor lay motionless, ice-cold beads of sweat trickling round his torso.

In the wood, Hamish, Lachlan, Colin and Alan waited with bated breath. The sounds of the advancing enemy grew louder and louder. They waited for the uproar that would tell them that Gregor was discovered. The atmosphere was electric. They could neither retreat over the river, nor could they fight their way out, hopelessly outnumbered as they would be. All they could hope for was an honourable end, taking as many Redcoats with them as they could. They waited. The noise of the advancing men seemed only feet away. Then it started to diminish.

Gregor lay face down in the ditch, relying on his filthy plaid to camouflage his prostrate form. The temptation to tense himself for action was nearly overwhelming. Marching feet passed within inches. He could not only hear the Redcoats, he literally could smell them, a strange mixture of sweat and unwashed bodies, of stale ale and tobacco. As the noise lessened and the footsteps moved farther and farther away, he could hardly believe his luck. Only when total silence had reigned for several minutes did he stir. Then, like a phantom, he rose, floated across the road and was absorbed into the trees.

Once the tension of the past few minutes had melted away, Hamish acted. Arguing to himself that there was practically no danger of a second patrol following hard on the heels of the other, he motioned to his two companions and, together, they closed up on the road and slipped across one by one. They had arranged to re-group just above the tree-line several hundred feet and a couple of miles up the hillside. This proved difficult, and the dawn was nearly on them when, at last, all six were together again. The long spell of fine weather was obviously coming to a close. The air was heavy, and, to the west dark, thick clouds were rolling ominously. Rain could not be far off, somewhere between a blessing and a curse. The poor visibility would help the six to keep out of sight but the bleak hills ahead offered virtually no shelter when they stopped.

Their route took them south, high up on Drumashie Moor, running parallel with the military road in the Great Glen below. In this desolate spot, they reached a lochan and, beside it, a copse of ancient, stunted pines. Several of these had succumbed to the frequent westerly gales, had been uprooted, yet, with amazing tenacity, continued to grow, albeit more horizontally than vertically. It was here, in the shelter of these fallen trees, that the clansmen settled down to spend the daylight hours. It was perilously close to the heavily patrolled Wade road but was the best they could find in the time available. They ate the last of the mutton and took turns to sleep and to keep watch. The expected rain came, noisily accompanied by peals of thunder that echoed and re-echoed around the encircling hills. Visibility dropped to a few yards as the rain came down in torrents. Glad they were in some sort of shelter, the six men could only hope that the downpour would at least ease by evening. However, it did not. Instead, it seemed to increase, if that were possible. Remaining under cover was tempting. However, with their foes only a mile or so away and, with no food and no prospect of getting any, staying put was not a realistic option. March they must, so march they did. Eastwards past Loch Duntelchaig, then south-east into the deep recesses of the Mondaliaths, shrouded in their plaids, swept by sheets of rain, they marched. Because of the rain, the evening was unnaturally dark, enabling them to set off several hours earlier than they otherwise would, which was just as well because by midnight it was too dark to continue.

By then the clansmen had found a hidden corrie far from any human habitation. This isolation was no great blessing, however. There was not so much as a ruined shieling to give them any respite from the rain. No doubt, if they lit a fire, its glow would be undetected, but there was no fuel. At least, no dry fuel. The peat all around them was potential fuel, but the rains had reduced it to a bog. All they did find was a huge boulder projecting ten feet out of the heather, with just enough overhang to provide some shelter. Groping around in the darkness, they gathered enough small rocks to provide a wind-break. Then, huddling together under their sodden plaids, they tried to forget their hunger and to get some sleep.

Chapter 20

Dawn came late to the corrie, if, indeed, it came at all. The clouds, dense and black, shrouded the surrounding mountains. The rain fell in unrelenting torrents. What daylight did filter through the clouds produced a dark, grey twilight. Only pressing hunger pangs and the sheer discomfort of their inadequate shelter motivated the men to rouse themselves. Wordlessly, they rose. With no breakfast to delay them, they were soon on the march again. The next hours took on a nightmarish quality. They climbed out of the corrie into the mist and rain of the desolate wilderness that they knew stretched for miles ahead of them and on both sides. Behind them, no doubt, was human habitation not too far away in the glens below, but there could be no going back. The safest, and indeed, the only practicable thing to do was to head for the McPherson lands in Badenoch far to the south. One last terrible march and they could be among friends.

Navigation was difficult in the extreme. The clouds were so thick that above was only a uniform charcoal grey giving no guidance from the sun. Direction-finding was a crude mix of half-remembered land-marks and a kind of sixth sense born of years of experience of the hills and the glens. The six walked on in silence. In no way could their progress now be described as a march. They stumbled over the peat-hags, forded the burns, scrambled across the rocks, sometimes feeling confident of their position, often, frankly, quite lost. No longer did they worry about security. Any Redcoats up here would be in an even worse state than themselves. Apart from which, two bands of men could pass within a hundred yards of each other and be completely oblivious of the other's presence.

As the crow flies, twenty-five miles would bring them to warmth, food and friends. But they were not crows. Every stream was now a dark brown raging torrent, so peat-stained that it was impossible to guess the depth of the occasional stretch of nearly still water and, at any of the many cataracts, so rapid that fording was well-nigh impossible. Repeatedly, they detoured up-stream, sometimes by miles, until they found a safe crossing. By late afternoon it was clear that they must spend another night on the hills. Reluctantly, Hamish guided the party eastwards, following the course of a swollen burn, loosing height rapidly. Nevertheless, it was more than two miles before they reached what might be called the tree-line. Such trees as there were, were stunted pines and rowans, growing wherever they could find some shelter from the prevailing westerly winds. The ground underfoot was alternately bog - every step being ankle-deep in the spongy peat - or it was rock. Every depression in the ground was a puddle, each of indeterminate depth and each having to be skirted lest it be deep enough to swallow a man without trace.

Finding a fallen pine, they decided to make a camp there. With swords and dirks, the six hacked branches off surrounding trees to form a crude shelter, using the stout trunk of the fallen tree as a roof-ridge. Having made a sufficient frame-work of the branches, they then thatched it with heather. The resulting shelter was nearly totally water-tight so far as the rain was concerned. The ground under foot was more liquid than solid, so more branches and more heather were cut until at last a cabin that, at a squeeze, could just accommodate all six, was complete. It kept out most of the rain and cut the draught from the gusting wind, but it did not keep out the cold. Hunger and exhaustion reduced the men to a shivering huddle. Despite their fatigue, sleep was elusive. Every joint seemed to ache mercilessly. Their sodden plaids provided little comfort. There was no conversation. Each man thought of tomorrow, knowing they would either win through or die. There was no hope of surviving another such night without food and warmth.

All night long the rain poured down. Day-light brought no relief. The dark clouds above conspired with the mists around to produce a kind of eerie half-light. The thunder of the burn in spate made conversation difficult. Wearily, drawing on their last reserves of strength, the six men stumbled to their feet. At a slow, relentless pace they trudged, until about mid-day the mist lifted slightly as they crossed a high ridge. Below them lay a familiar sight, the broad strath, the brown, deep loch, the tumbling burn, and, beyond, the crags of the massive Creag nan Uamh. It seemed to Hamish an age since he had struggled up this very glen with the uncomplaining Davie. Guiltily, he realised that in the busyness of recent days, he had hardly spared a thought for his cousin. Was he alive and mending fast? Or had the horrific injuries carried him off?

Even as they stood there, the weather closed in again and the strath below vanished behind curtains of rain and the cloud came down again. Four miles. Perhaps two hours. Then warmth, shelter, food and friends! With new energy fuelled by hope, the six plunged off down a steep scree-slope that terminated in thigh-deep, saturated heather in the corrie below. No discomfort could dampen their spirits now and enthusiastically they headed for the burn that tumbled out of the loch.

Chapter 21

As they drew near, the full reality of the spate came home to Hamish. The normally gentle trout stream had broken its banks and was nearly two hundred yards wide, an oppressively dark, swift flowing flood. Farther down, its waters narrowed as they were compressed by the restricting mouth of the glen. The usually fordable burn was now a serious obstacle. Where, in more normal times, it leapt from one rock pool to another, providing a dozen or more places where a child could skip across dry-shod, it was now a thundering cataract, throwing spray into the air like smoke. And still the rain fell remorselessly down. Suddenly feeling desperately tired, Hamish peered through the rain and the mist back up the foaming river. The loch was barely in sight. With no boat, it was impassable. Beyond it, though hidden in the mist and the rain, the burn that fed it tumbled down in a torrent from the crags above, every bit as unfordable as the cascade lower down. It was a straight choice. Cross below the loch, where the water was wide but of unknown depth, or climb back right out of the glen, skirt round the top of the corrie with its myriad feeder burn, swollen but passable, and descend the other side. One mile, no climbing, but a hazardous river crossing. Or eight miles, 1800 feet to ascend and descend, but infinitely less danger. Calling his five friends round him he summed it up.

"Under normal circumstances we would cross here, knee-deep at most. Now! Well you can see for yourselves. We could be up to our waists or even deeper. And there's the cask to bear in mind too! Alternatively, it's back up the hill. A hard, hard slog, but we should make it by night-fall. Even if we are overtaken by dark, I'm on familiar ground and we'll get there safely." Gregor was shivering so much he could hardly speak.

"I don't think I'm fit for the roundabout route," he said, "I'm just about done for as it is. Let's take our chances with the stream."

The other four murmured their agreement.

"Why not hide the cask this side," said Lachlan. "We will get across much easier without it. It will be safe enough here and we can recover it tomorrow when we've fed and slept."

On the whole, this seemed good sense, although it was with profound reluctance that Hamish concealed the heavy burden in the cleft between two rocks. He glanced round anxiously but the mist had closed in and no prying eyes could possibly see the hiding place. Two hundred yards from the burn and fifty feet above it, the cache was safe even should the waters rise yet higher.

The six entered the waters gingerly, in pairs. Supporting one another and probing the bed ahead of them with their swords, lest they fall into a hole, they waded out into the surging stream. Knee-deep, thigh-deep, waist-deep, fighting to keep their balance against the forceful current. Step by painful step, the waters now nearly to their chests. Then almost imperceptibly, uphill. The water level dropped to their waists once more. However, as it became shallower, the force of the current increased. Suddenly Gregor stumbled and fell so abruptly that he lost his grasp of Alan. He disappeared under the coffee-brown flood to emerge fifteen yards downstream, coughing and struggling. Alan threw off his plaid and unhesitatingly plunged in after his friend, swimming strongly down-stream. Lachlan and Colin in front were almost at the far shore and, with a tremendous extra effort, pulled themselves up on to bank. Casting aside their swords and their plaids, they dashed off through the mist. Run as fast as they would, however, they could not catch up with the two men who were being swept along by the accelerating water and were nearing the maelstrom ahead. Alan had nearly reached Gregor when the latter fetched up headfirst against a rock with a fearful crack. Alan grabbed his inert body and tried to swim to shore. It was too late and, to the horror of the men running down the bank, both rescuer and rescued plunged into the steaming abyss.

Making a wide detour to by-pass the falls, Colin and Lachlan leapt from boulder to boulder to arrive at relatively calm water nearly quarter of a mile below. Up and down they searched, aided by Hamish and Jamie who had by now joined them. After a fruitless hour in which all they had found was Gregor's plaid caught on a projecting rock, they had to face up to the harsh truth. Their friends were gone forever. Hamish sat down on a boulder, feeling utterly drained. He had now lost four men, half his little command. More than that, he had lost four friends. True, he had known some of them only a few short days, but shared hardships forge unbreakable bonds between men. Tears flooded his eyes and he felt as never before like giving up.

The other three gathered round, shock and sorrow lining each face. Without a word, Hamish rose to his feet and led the way back up the hill, above the falls, off to the right, and up the scree-slope. The rain hid their approach to the cave and likewise the cave's mouth from their sight. However the whiff of peat-smoke told them it was occupied. Obviously no look-out had been posted, hardly surprising, as the chances of a Government patrol so far from civilisation were negligible. Calling the password, Hamish scrambled down into the shadows of the cave, to be greeted by Rory.

"Hamish! I heard Cluny had left you with Locheil! You're the last man I ever expected to drop in like this!"

"How's Davie?" panted Hamish, half hoping, half dreading the answer.

"Just fine! Just fine!" came Davie's familiar voice from the darker shadows of the cave. "Not on my feet yet, but mending fast! And it's all thanks to you."

Embarrassed, Hamish brushed the thanks aside.

"Any food?" he demanded. "We've not eaten for three days and we're ravenous."

Well, you're in luck," replied Rory. "Cluny restocked us only yesterday. You mind Callum, yon tall lad with the broken arm we brought up here? Well he's made an excellent recovery and insisted on going back to Badenoch with Cluny's men. So there's plenty. Smoked venison. Salt beef. Smoked salmon. Take your choice."

And eat they did, as only starving men can. Then, still wrapped in their steaming plaids, they snuggled down by the glowing peats and slept. For over twelve hours they slept, then rose, ate and dozed again. Outside, it still rained.

Chapter 22

Early in the afternoon, Hamish stood at the cave mouth and peered through the mist and the rain-squalls.

"Lachlan," he said, "we really must make the effort to bring in that cask. It's tempting to wait for better weather, but, if we do, we run the risk of a patrol spotting us in the open and then it'll be all up for every single one of us."

"Aye! Let's get on with it. We will have to go round by the tops. What do you think? Eight or nine miles each way? We'll be comfortably back by dusk."

So they set off. Amazing what a difference a full stomach and a good night's rest make, thought Hamish as the two marched in single file, climbing steeply, but still covering the ground at some four miles an hour. The head of the corrie passed, the two lost height rapidly, descending through the dense mist to arrive with unerring accuracy at the hiding place. A pessimistic streak in Hamish led him to expect the wretched cask for which so much good blood had been shed to have disappeared. It had not. Undisturbed, it lay where they had left it what seemed weeks ago but was, in reality, a bare twenty-four hours earlier. Hoisting to his shoulder Hamish turned on his heel and strode off back up the mountain. Apart from even more ferocious than usual squalls of rain, their return journey was as uneventful as the outward-bound one. In growing darkness, the evening shadows falling unseasonably early due to the heavy cloud and monsoon-like rain, they arrived back at the cave, soaked to the skin but satisfied. They carried the cask to the deepest part of the cave and gratefully laid it down.

The interior of the cave was a haven of smoky warmth. The two stripped off their dripping clothes and soon their rapidly drying plaids were adding to the moist, warm fug. More food and more sleep. Then Hamish would decide whether to move on to Ben Alder, or rest up for a day or two more.

When Hamish did wake, a feeble, watery light filtered in from the mouth of the cave. The fire was almost out; only a wisp of blue smoke was curling up from the embers. Everybody else was asleep. Colin and Lachlan had seemed none the worst for the adventures and privations of the last few days. He was more anxious about Jamie, however. The lad was feverish the night before last, shivering uncontrollably. Some of this was no doubt due to fatigue and hunger. No small part would be due to shock. The tragedy of losing Gregor and Alan so close to safety had appalled them all, but Jamie had taken the loss even harder than the others. Guilt sat as a heavy burden on Hamish himself. He had taken a risk and those two had paid the price. No matter that the other five had all agreed with the decision, ultimate responsibility was his. Miserable, he rose quietly to his feet and climbed to the mouth of the cave. Keeping hard up against the massive rock that hid the cave from the view of anyone in the glen below, he looked out cautiously through the driving rain at the desolate scene both up and down the glen. Nothing stirred. The feeble daylight reflected back from the puddles that had accumulated in every hollow. The loch was slate-grey, its surface one minute flat, the next whipped up by a passing squall. There seemed little or no chance of the Government troops penetrating so deeply into such an unpopulated region, but, for all that, Hamish decided that they had better maintain a watch. Although passing soldiers would not suspect the presence of the cave itself, the fragrant smell of peat-smoke might alert them to the presence of the fugitives. Early warning would ensure that the fire could be put out and complete silence maintained. There was no need to trouble the others. Wrapping his plaid round him, he settled down under the overhang of the rock out of the hissing rain.

The morning dragged on and it was towards noon before Lachlan joined him.

"They are all awake now," he said. "Rory's making porridge. Do you want some?"

"Aye, and thanks, Lachlan. I wonder if we should press on today? There's no sign of a let-up in the weather. I can't remember when it last rained so hard and for so long at this time of year. Do you think young Jamie's fit to go? It will take at least two more days to reach Ben Alder. The Badenoch area's bound to be crawling with Redcoats, so most of the journey will have to be done at night and it will be desperately slow. No fires to dry out by, cold meals only. What do you think?"

"I didn't like the look of Jamie yesterday, but I think he's looking brighter this morning. Davie's on the mend, but I'm worried about Rory's other patient. Colin helped change his bandages while we were away yesterday. A bayonet has hacked a terrible hole in his thigh and the wound is awfully inflamed. He's in a high fever and if the poison runs all through him, he'll never make it."

"Sad, but not our problem," said Hamish. "We ought to press on as soon as ever we can. If Rory can't help him, no-one can. Staying here won't do any good."

"Aye, but if he does die, who's to bury him? Rory and Davie could barely drag a big lad like that out of the cave, let alone carry him a mile or two away and dig a reasonable grave. If they can't take him far, sooner or later, the soldiers will find his remains and it will then be only a matter of time before they find the cave too. Then it'll be all up for Davie and Rory."

The harsh realism of this assessment hit Hamish like a physical blow.

"Right enough," he replied. "We'd better hold off for a day or two. He'll either start to mend or he won't within that time. Have you fed?"

"Aye, you go and eat and I'll stand guard here," came the reply.

Hamish slipped back into the cave. Dave and Rory were eating. Jamie was awake, lying on his back and gazing unseeingly at the craggy ceiling above. Beyond him, the fevered form of the wounded highlander lay, swathed in plaids, but shivering convulsively. It wasn't difficult to understand Lachlan's concern. To Hamish's unskilled eye, it looked as though the end could not be far off. The fevered man tossed and turned. As he did so, he muttered deliriously. Hamish turned away as sadness, like a black cloud, descended on him. He did not know the fellow, but no doubt many others did. No doubt he was loved. Somewhere, anxious relatives would be waiting apprehensively for his return. Perhaps a wife. Perhaps children. Or ageing parents.

These all, not merely deprived of one they loved, but deprived too of the family breadwinner without whom only a grey and desolate road of hardship and poverty would lie ahead of them in this life. And this was a story being repeated in every glen throughout the Highlands of Scotland. The immediate aftermath of the defeat at Culloden had cost thousands of lives already, but a fearful further cull of the ordinary folk over the coming winter and beyond was inevitable.

Chapter 23

Lachlan, Hamish and Colin shared the sentry duty, each standing watch for about an hour at a time. The rain continued, now accompanied by dramatic flashes of lightning and almost continuous peals of thunder. There was little to do but rest and, sporadically, to talk. The fevered man rambled on from time to time, talking and groaning as he lapsed in and out of consciousness. Jamie slept most of the afternoon. Colin was on watch and Davie and Hamish were talking quietly late in the afternoon when a noise like a thousand cannon firing at once crashed through the cave. Everything went dark. Thick dust filled the air and the two were choking and gasping for breath. Catching his plaid to his mouth to filter out the worst of the dust, Hamish groped his way towards the cave mouth. Only it was no longer there! Rocks and pebbles rolled down towards him, whilst choking dust swirled around. The gloom was broken only by the glow of the fire and, farther back in the cave, the flickering flame of a small lamp.

"A rock-fall," gasped Lachlan. "The doorway's blocked off completely."

Hamish tried to reply but his words trailed off in a fit of uncontrollable, body-racking coughing. He wrapped his plaid over his head and shoulders and tried to bring his tortured throat under control. Meanwhile Lachlan had scrambled up the loose shale to where the mouth of the cave had been. With his bare hands, he pulled at some of the smaller stones, but, to his despair he soon realised that the entrance was blocked by a mass of boulders, each weighing tons. He slid back down to where Davie and Hamish were.

"We're blocked in," he said, somewhat unnecessarily. "We'd better get the fire out so it does not suffocate us."

So saying he picked up the water container and poured the entire contents on the smouldering embers. The darkness seemed the more profound, only the small lamp giving a little light.

"Can we not dig round the rocks?" demanded Davie.

He scrambled up and poked and probed with a dirk. Five minutes later he gave up.

"You might manage to roll the stones away from outside, but it's impossible to do anything from within," he reported. "Never mind, Colin's out there and when he sees what's happened he'll get some of Cluny's folk and they'll get us out."

"Aye, but not before tomorrow," said Lachlan. "Meanwhile we will have to sit tight and not use up any more air than necessary. The fire is still smouldering slightly. Help me stamp it out."

So saying, he kicked the remaining glowing peats until the last spark was extinguished.

"Now we wait for Colin to bring help," said Hamish with a confidence he did not feel.

He tried to silence that part of his mind that kept asking just where Colin would have been when the land-slide began. The chances of his escaping sudden death were remote, unless the lad had strayed a bit from the cave-mouth to stretch his legs. If he had been caught in the fall, they were all doomed. It would be days before Cluny sent fresh supplies. If the hillside were sufficiently altered, it might be well nigh impossible to know where to dig. With a determined effort, he pushed these thoughts out of his mind.

So the six men settled down to wait for Colin to go for help. But Colin was not going anywhere. He had been sitting under the overhang, sheltering from the ever-present rain, idly making patterns in the ground in front of him with a gigantic claymore that he had found among the various other swords and guns concealed in the cave. A shower of small pebbles and rocks from above pattered down around him and he looked up just in time to see a vast slab of rock, bigger than a barn, hurtle towards him. His curiosity had less than a second to turn to raw, naked fear when the rock cannoned on to the rock he was sheltering beside. It drove this rock down the scree-slope, shattering into a thousand pieces as it did so. One minor shard of stone neatly detached the rear quarter of his skull, propelling him from time into eternity. Dead, his body was buried in seconds by the myriad of smaller pebbles that followed the main fall. The thunderous noise of the rock-fall echoed around the glen, reverberating in a diminuendo that eventually fell away to nothing and, apart from the constant hiss of the rain, silence reigned. If the cave was well hidden before, no one would remotely guess its presence now.

Chapter 24

Down in the deep shadows below, the men waited for rescue that would never come. Hamish's eyes became more accustomed to the gloom and he sat motionless, thinking of his home, his parents, his friends. He glanced at the stoical Davie, who also sat in silence. Not for the first time Hamish wondered if he had really done his cousin any favour, extending his life by these pain-filled days and nights since Culloden. A man can only do what seems right at the time, he told himself severely. If he had his time again, he would do exactly the same. Now they faced almost certain death together once again. He could not ask to die in better company.

Rory was bending over his patient. Hamish realised that there had been not a sound from the poor fellow for more than an hour. Rory straightened up, pulled a plaid over the man's face and sadly shook his head.

"It's all over for him," he said. "I'd hoped that, having survived this far, he might yet have pulled through. However it was not to be."

Lachlan and Jamie were talking in low tones, but Hamish could not make out a word. They had done so well, the two of them, enduring hardship and danger without a murmur. They had accepted his authority and loyally carried out his decisions without question. And now it had come to this, trapped alive in a tomb hidden from the sight of all, a slow lingering death. Yet he did not rebuke himself. This was not a situation of his making. In no sense was it his fault. Indeed it was no-one's fault, only one of the unforeseeable fortunes of war.

A couple of hours later, all conversation ceased. The men tried to eat, but appetites had gone. The all-pervasive dust contaminated all the food and they were already regretting the use of all the water when the fire was put out. There was a small flask of French brandy. Each man took a mouthful, feeling the raw spirit burn its way down into their stomachs. With nothing else to do the five rolled themselves in their plaids and, rather surprisingly, slept.

Sleep was not relaxing for Hamish. Again and again he woke, shuddering from one nightmare after another. Each time he struggled into wakefulness, not remembering the dream, yet strangely still haunted by its faded memory. There was now no way of distinguishing night from day. He slept, yet had no way of knowing whether he had been unconscious for minutes or hours. At one point, he pulled himself erect, strangely light-headed. Breathing was becoming more difficult. His lungs burnt and his throat was raw. None of the others stirred. He listened in the oppressive silence. One or two were breathing, but breathing with difficulty and gasping with every breath. He was not sure if all of them were still breathing.

Even standing was difficult. He found himself swaying uncertainly. He lay down again and fell asleep. Suddenly, he was back at Culloden. All around him was noise. The shout of command. The thunder of cannon. The whistle of grapeshot. The rattle of muskets. And above it all, the unforgettable sound of wounded men shrieking in agony, men - some highlanders, some Irish [for many Irish fought and died for the Prince and the Jacobite cause]. There were the enemy wounded as well, a mixed bag of English, German and Scots, these latter mainly Lowlanders, although several Highland clans, notably the execrated Campbells, had fought for the Hanovarian King George. The noise, yes, and the smell of conflict. The reek of cordite and of blood and entrails, both human and horse. Hamish was wielding his sword again. Then his feet went from under him. He was down. A gigantic soldier towered above him. A bayonet plunged into his breast. Searing pain ran like fire through his chest. He groped his way back to wakefulness. The scenes and sounds of battle faded. A total silence filled the cave. Only the burning pain in his chest was real. He gasped for breath. His eyes focused on the guttering candle. It was burning with a feeble, yellow flame and emitting an evil, black smoke. He tried to sit up. Everything went red, then black and he sank back onto his plaid.

A couple of hours later the candle gave a final splutter and went out.

Book 3

Chapter 1
3rd MAY 1996

The old man stirred in his hospital bed. How long had he been here? It seemed an age ago that strong but caring hands had helped him into the ambulance. Of his arrival in Inverness, he remembered nothing. Slowly he had come to some semblance of consciousness, more often, however, hovering somewhere between wakefulness and a twilight world of dreams and nightmares. The drugs had brought the pain under control, but had brought with them this terrible inability to concentrate and the problem of sorting out the real from the imaginary.

Today he felt better, as though he had passed some important milestone on the road to full recovery. Doctors and nurses alike had been kindness itself and, much as he disliked hospitals, he reluctantly admitted to himself that, if he must be in one, Raigmore would be hard to beat. The doctor came to his bedside as she made her routine daily round of her patients.

"Well, and how's our Mr McPherson this morning?" she asked, with a smile that lit up her whole face. "You're looking better! How do you feel?

"Much better, thanks. I'm breathing more easily and the pain is nearly all gone. You've all been so kind that I don't want to complain, but the nightmares! I sleep all night, but I'm exhausted by morning. I know they're only dreams but they're so realistic that I've difficulty knowing what's real anymore."

"Now you know what a druggie means when he talks about a 'bad trip'! It's the drugs, I'm afraid. Some people react like that and, I'm sorry, but we can do little about it. The good news is that we're cutting the dosage and by the weekend you'll be off them completely. Now, I want you to get up as much as you feel able. It's much better for your chest if you are erect and moving around. Take it easy to begin with. From here to the day-room will be quite far enough to begin with. Go and watch some television. Just don't overdo things to begin with and I'll see you again tomorrow."

She started to go, then turned.

"You really were very naughty not to call your doctor earlier. You gave us all a nasty fright. I really thought we were going to lose you. Don't let it happen again!"

Only her infectious smile took the edge off her words and the old man smiled gratefully back. He had been an obstinate fool. With a final wave, the doctor disappeared round the curtain that screened his bed.

Later, McPherson, with a pretty young nurse at his elbow, shuffled the few steps to the day-room. He did not watch much television. Whoever described it as 'chewing gum for the eyes' had summed it up quite well, he considered, although he would grudgingly admit to enjoying some historical documentaries. Now he had timed his visit to catch the BBC news. It was three weeks and more since he had last seen a news programme. Not that he would have missed much, he reflected. When you get past seventy, you feel you've seen it all before. He'd sometimes thought about publishing a spoof scientific paper expounding the view that all history was cyclical. Everything that happened had happened before. If history were only accurately recorded over, say, the last 2000 years, you would see that there was nothing new under the sun. Publish in the name of some unpronounceable [but fictitious] Russian professor and you would probably win a doctorate for the mythical fellow!

He settled down to listen to the latest. Sex scandals in high places. Same as usual, only the names change. The essential salacious details that do so much for circulation and viewing figures remain monotonously similar. Terrorist bombings. Where this time? Beirut? Northern Ireland? Some American embassy? Will the skins of the pathetic casualties be black, brown or white? All else remains much the same. Human anguish is the same the world-over. Tragedy is colour-blind. Suffering is the great leveller, hurting rich and poor, black and white, with callous lack of discrimination. The announcer droned on and the old man drifted in and out of sleep. Then, suddenly, there was that cave that had so hunted his recent dreams! Was he dreaming now? No! The picture was there on the screen. A rather indistinct shot, downwards at the pile of dull gold coins scattered on a rocky floor.

"At 9.30 this evening, we have a special edition of 'Scottish History Revisited', with Hubert Macmillan, the eminent expert on the Jacobite Rebellion. For the very first time, a series of pictures that have been given on permanent loan to the Scottish Museum Archives will be included. Mr Macmillan explores the subject 'Bonnie Prince Charlie's Gold: The Legend Lives On'. Do not miss this programme with its startling new evidence about one of the most intriguing incidents in this country's complex history. The programme contains several pictures that some viewers may find distressing."

"I'm sure they just say that to boost the viewing figures," muttered the patient in the next chair. "Anyway, they'll have us all tucked up in bed by then, so we can't watch it even if we want to."

Nodding a farewell, McPherson rose stiffly to his feet. He made it back to bed, just. Feeling drained, he leant back gratefully on the pillows. He must see that programme, but how? He beckoned to one of the nurses.

"Do you think I can sit up until 10 to watch a TV programme?" he asked. "It's of special interest to me and I don't want to miss it."

"I'll speak to sister," came the reply, "but don't hold your breath! She's a real stickler and I don't give much for your chances. Don't you have someone at home who can record it for you?"

"No," said McPherson sadly. "No-one. I live alone and have no near relatives."

Ten minutes later she was back.

"As I thought, no chance," she reported. "The old battle-axe wouldn't hear of it. One trip a day to the day-room is quite enough for you. Besides, she says, it'll create a principle and patients will be wanting to stay up all the hours to watch whatever they fancy.

"I'm sorry, but I did try."

"Well, thanks anyway. I'm sure you did your best."

And, with a smile she left. Perhaps the programme will be repeated sometime, mused McPherson as he dozed off.

Chapter 2

Just before 9.30 the sister bustled up. Producing a very small portable television set, she placed it on the table in front of him.

"Now, just make sure you keep the volume down," she said gruffly. McPherson smiled and thanked her profusely.

"Mind, only until 10, and not a minute after!" And with that she swept away like a galleon with every sail set.

"Careful, lassie," muttered the grateful patient, "you very nearly smiled then!"

Over the next half-hour, he relived the whole cave experience. His heart swelled with pride at the graphic illustrations. Considering the circumstances, his photographs were amazing. The focus was almost always good, the real disappointments being the shots taken at long range of the gold coins. You could see they were coins and that the colour was yellow, but that was about all. The ones of the corpses were indeed distressingly real. 'The stuff that dreams are made of' McPherson whispered to himself. Well, nightmares, actually.

The commentary was inane and, somewhat inevitably, highly speculative. The only surprising thing was a reference to the cave being in Moidart. Where that had come from, he could not begin to guess. The bulk of the programme was taken up with a highly sensationalised account of the supply of French gold for the Pretender's cause. All in all, it was a good fifteen minutes' worth. The pity was that it lasted thirty minutes!

Promptly, at 10, he switched off. He slid down the bed and, for the first time since he visited the cave, he slept a deep and dreamless sleep. He woke alert, refreshed. It was as if the ghosts of the cave had been exorcised and at last he could put the matter behind him. Then the cheery WVS volunteer came with the day's papers. Headlines screamed, "The Hunt for the Gold Is On". "Burial at Culloden for Cave Heroes?" "State Funeral With Military Honours?" He bought four different papers.

He read in horror. The Nationalists were demanding a state funeral and a national memorial. One of the tabloids was offering a colossal sum of money to the first one to find the cave. The Church was on the band-wagon, with a popular clergyman demanding a Christian burial in hallowed ground. Even the one 'quality' paper enthused about 'this important contribution of our understanding of our nation's history'. The only comfort was that 'the source of the film remained a closely guarded secret'. How long that would last was anyone's guess.

At visiting time McPherson did have a visitor, the first since his admission to Raigmore, Robert Macrae, the former pupil and friend to whom he had entrusted the photographs. The younger man was writhing with embarrassment.

"I tried to consult you a couple of weeks ago but was told you were not seeing visitors. I contacted a neighbour who is a professor in the Edinburgh medical school and he spoke to a consultant here who had been one of his students. I don't know how to tell you this, but he said you would be dead before the programme went out."

"I always was unreliable," replied McPherson with a grin, "and I did say to do what you liked with them, so I can hardly complain! I only hope I'm not going to be persecuted by the media."

"I've given nothing away. I even accidentally on purpose let slip something about Moidart. I withdrew it immediately, but the more I said it was a slip of the tongue, the more certain the news-hounds became that that was where to look! Every hotel from Fort William to Mallaig ought to be paying me a commission!" said Robert, with a mischievous grin.

"Perhaps some good may yet come out of this, if there is a genuine revival of interest in the causes and effects of the '45. Far too many people just assume it was a straight 'Scots versus English' affair, instead of something more akin to a Scottish civil war. I wonder, for instance, how many folk realise that six Scottish regiments fought for King George at Culloden? I only hope that these newspapers do nothing to stir up old hatreds. You've only to look across at Ireland to see what that might do."

"I don't think you need worry about that," said the younger man. "The Scots have never shown a tendency to nurture such grudges. It's a bit surprising, really, when you think that Culloden was half a century nearer our time than the Battle of the Boyne. Add to that what the Highland Scots suffered in the aftermath of the '45 and then the 19th Century clearances, when crofters were hounded out of the lands they and their forebears had tilled for centuries to make way for sheep."

"Aye, but taking that point first. For the most part, it was Scots landlords who evicted Scots crofters. Sheer human greed! Greed that is there in every race and nation, I'm afraid.

"The other point is more complex, I think," he continued. "Right enough, after all they had suffered, you might have thought that right down to the present day the highland clans might have wanted to strike back at the Lowlanders and the English. I sometimes wonder if the religious revivals of the 19th century didn't play a greater part in producing a lasting peace than many people realise."

"Religion doesn't seemed to have done the Irish much good!" exclaimed Robert.

"True," came the reply, "but, in the Highlands, religion was much more of a spiritual thing, not political. I think that is the big difference. The ordinary folk primarily were taken up with their relationship with their God rather than with their southern neighbours, Scots or English. It is perhaps significant that the Bible was not translated into Gaelic until the beginning of the 18th century, nearly a hundred years after the English speaking world got the Scriptures in their every-day language. The spiritual revival under the Wesleys and the Methodists swept England a hundred years and more after the ordinary folk got the King James Bible. It is interesting to note that revival swept through the Scottish Highlands a hundred years or so after the coming of the Gaelic Bible."

"I hadn't thought of that," said Robert. "It is generally reckoned that one of the important effects of the Wesleyan revival in England was that the English did not follow the French example at the time of the French Revolution. Perhaps, similarly, the highland clansmen became preoccupied with their spiritual state and reconciled to the hardships inflicted on them. Talk about religion being the opiate of the people!"

"Don't knock it, unless you would prefer a Scotland with Northern Ireland's problems!"

"To change the subject, somewhat," resumed Robert, "I've been asked to take part in a televised debate next week. Apparently there is doubt being cast on the authenticity of your photos and someone has come up with idea that it's all a big hoax."

"It might be best if that were the conclusion reached and then the whole thing can die a death. I really can't see any good coming out of it and I really dread the press discovering who took the pictures."

"I don't think you need worry on that score, said Robert. "I'll put up yet more of a smoke-screen. Only you and I know the truth and if we're both careful they'll never find out."

"I wish I shared your optimism," came the gloomy reply. "Once they start to dig they usually come up with something. Anyway, I'll watch your programme with great interest. I'm so glad you came to see me. You've cheered me up no end."

The two chatted on for half an hour more. After Robert had left, McPherson lay back in bed. He still tired easily, but at heart he felt so much better. The next three days, indeed, saw a tremendous difference in him. His pains were completely gone. His breathing was normal and his general sense of well-being excellent. Indeed, he was soon chafing to be back in his own cottage. The nurses were superb. Even the 'old battle-axe' of a sister would pause to chat to him. But, for all their friendliness, he wanted to be back home.

Chapter 3

On the fourth day, the doctor came on her regular round. She examined him with even greater care than usual.

"I don't know how this ward is going to manage without you," she said with a smile, "but, after tomorrow, it's just going to have to try! Yes! You can go home. Mind you look after your self, though. The slightest pain, difficulty in breathing or anything else, you phone the doctor. Now, do you promise?"

By now McPherson would have made any promise. All he wanted was the peace and the familiar surroundings of his own home. Soon, however, the formidable sister hove into view. Why can I only think of her in nautical terms? He wondered idly. She swept up to his bed.

"What have you been up to now?" she demanded. "There are four reporters laden down with cameras all wanting to see you. Do you want to see them? I certainly don't want them traipsing all over my ward."

"Please, please chase them away. All I want is peace!" he replied weakly.

"Fine, but they seem awfully keen. I think they will just picket the place and nobble you when you leave tomorrow. Anyway, I'll get the porters to keep them at bay for now." So saying she bustled away.

The rest of that day seemed to drag on endlessly. In late afternoon, he was half asleep when a white-coated figure with a stethoscope protruding from the pocket sat beside his bed.

"Hello, we've not met before, have we?" said McPherson, looking his visitor up and down. She was young and she was pretty, almost beautiful, he thought. Are doctors really as young as that nowadays? She looked slightly awkward and almost embarrassed so he tried to put her at her ease.

"I don't know if they've told you, but I'm going home tomorrow. I am almost tempted to have a relapse if you're to be my doctor!"

The girl blushed.

"I'm not a doctor. I'm from the 'Scottish Reporter' newspaper. The porter wouldn't let me in to see you, so I borrowed the coat and stethoscope and just marched in as if I owned the place. Amazing what you can get away with if you try! Anyway, I'm authorised to offer you £20,000 for an exclusive story on how you took the Prince Charlie's gold pictures. If you'll take a team of our photographers to the cave I think you can name your own price."

McPherson was aghast. How had she found him? How many others would be coming in her trail? Was this the end of his peace? He lay back, speechless and stunned.

"Please, Mr McPherson. Tell me you'll agree. I may not have much time. You will agree, won't you," and she switched on her most winning smile.

That did it for the old man! If there was one thing he disliked, it was someone trying to manipulate him and the idea that this young thing thought she had only to flutter her eyes at him and he would jump through hoops for her infuriated him.

"I can get £20,000 and more from the Daily Express with an exclusive about unscrupulous reporters from disreputable newspapers masquerading as doctors to squeeze information out of hospital patients. Besides, I'm sure the Press Complaints Commission will have something to say about this!"

"Oh! Mr McPherson, you wouldn't!" A look of genuine dismay crossed the woman's crimson face. "I so wanted this story. There's several more reporters outside and I did want to be first. Honestly, I didn't mean to upset you. You wouldn't report it, would you?"

McPherson put on his most implacable look, although part of him felt sorry for the silly woman.

"You wouldn't, would you she persisted." McPherson's hand reached for the bell-push. "You would! I'm in deep trouble now," she said almost in a whimper.

The old man relented. "Tell me how you found me and you can sneak out as you sneaked in," he said.

Relief flashed across her face.

"The chap who developed your pictures contacted me. He remembered them. They were hardly your usual family holiday snaps and he had wondered what the story behind them was. He gave me your name and it didn't take long to trace you to here."

"All right," said McPherson, "but if your rag publishes my name you'll never hear the end of it, believe me! Now, get out before I change my mind."

The chastened woman departed, leaving behind her a disturbed man. His hopes of returning to the peace and quiet of home were shattered. That woman might not be back, but if she could trace him, so could others. Not for the first time, he devoutly wished he had never set eyes on that wretched cave.

Chapter 4

An hour or so later, he telephoned Robert Macrae to update him on this latest development. Macrae was horrified.

"I suppose it was almost inevitable that they would trace you sooner or later, but I never imagined it would be so soon. The sheer nerve of that woman! Fancy walking in, cool as a cucumber like that! I really can't get over that. They'll follow you to Speyside too. I'm sorry but you'll get no peace."

"I'll be able to put up with that once I'm really fit, but I could do without it just now," said McPherson.

"Why not come and spend a week or two with us until things quieten down? Mary would just love to pamper you and the media can run circles round themselves in Aviemore and Kingussie. They won't think of looking for you in Edinburgh. I'm getting a fat fee for my television appearance. Come and help me spend my ill-gotten gains!"

"Thanks, I'd love to. You know I've no close relatives now. That's the price I pay for outliving them all! I've only a nephew and he's in London. No doubt he'd welcome me, but I just can't face the travel. Then there's all the bustle of South East England! Far too many people jammed into far too little space. No! I'm really grateful and I'd love to come. I'll phone you again when I've arranged things here."

"Marvellous! We'll look forward to having you. We'll have a great time and I'll be glad to get more background from you. Maybe one day when the fuss has all died down, you'll take me to the cave."

"No chance! Wild horses won't drag me up that hill again. Let the dead stay buried where they are! I wish I'd never gone near the place. However, the one thing you learn in life is that you can't turn the clock back! The greatest favour I can do for you is to keep you away from that chamber of horrors."

"If that's how you feel, so be it. I promise I won't ask again. You come, relax here and get yourself really better. Phone when you know your timetable. I can come up to Inverness and pick you up," said Robert.

"No! Thanks, but no! Too much risk of someone following you home. Leave it with me. I'll work something out."

The following morning the sister returned.

"We've an ambulance going to Perth to pick up a patient there. It'll drop you at Kingussie. The porter will be here shortly with a trolley. We'll get you on it and wheel you off to theatre with tubes sticking out everywhere. Then, when you're safely past the tripe-hounds, you can sneak out the back door and into the ambulance." She smiled, and all at once she not only looked human but she seemed to shed ten years or more.

"You're an angel!" said McPherson. "Mind you a pretty devious one, but an angel just the same! Thanks so much! I am so grateful for all you've done."

The sister blushed and hastily retired. Ten minutes a theatre trolley arrived, propelled by a young smiling porter.

"Your chariot awaits, sir," he grinned. "On you get and we'll soon have you out of here."

Two minutes later the trolley left the ward, the patient swathed in sheets and with an oxygen mask clamped over his face. After a sick-making journey through endless corridors the trolley stopped.

"All change! Transport for Perth through that door!" The jovial porter helped the old man off the trolley, out the door and into the waiting ambulance. The doors were shut and the journey began.

"You're going to Perth, dropping me off on the way?" asked McPherson.

"That's the general idea."

"Can I go all the way to Perth? If you could stop just long enough for me to throw one or two things into a suitcase, I'd be so grateful."

"Highly irregular, but why not? What've you been up to anyway. With all those media folk around the current theory is that you've robbed Fort Knox or something," said the driver as he accelerated southwards along the A9.

"Something like that," said McPherson, friendly enough, but discouraging further questions. In more or less complete silence they rolled on, and an hour later drew up outside the familiar cottage. It took only five minutes to pack a suitcase, then to make a quick call to Robert Macrae. All was organised. He would rendezvous with them at Perth Infirmary.

Everything went to plan. By evening, McPherson was sitting with Robert and Mary in the Macraes' comfortable lounge looking out over the River Forth. The next few days were spent in peaceful relaxation. McPherson needed no doctor to tell him he was getting better. Each day he walked a little farther than the day before. Each day he felt stronger.

Chapter 5

Then came the awaited television programme. It had, of course, been pre-recorded, so the three friends were able to settle down with a bottle of wine to watch it together. It started with a re-cap of the earlier programme, showing once again the best of McPherson's pictures. Then the discussion panel was introduced.

"First," said Jason Salmon, the chairman for the evening, "we're privileged to have Sir Montague Fraser, author, playwright and authority on all things Scottish." The dour, wiry little man in the kilt on his left attempted a friendly smile, but somehow it was still-born.

"Then the well-known Scots-Canadian, Mrs Shelagh Grant. Mrs Grant is renowned on both sides of the Atlantic for her research into the Highland Clearances and its contribution to the culture of Canada and Newfoundland." The mildly overweight, overdressed peroxide blonde squirmed in her seat, revealing her substantial legs. At least her smile was slightly more successful.

"And Professor Jean McAskill, of the Department of History and Ethnic Studies at Central University. Professor McAskill's book 'Gaels, Vikings and Celts: Three Cultures but One Nation', published earlier this year may be said to break new ground in early Scottish history." The aged face that was reminiscent of an ancient and much-used parchment broke into a smile that only accentuated its deep cracks and creases.

[Robert muttered, "Breaking new ground in exploring the ultimate limits of boredom, more like!"]

"Last, but not least, the man through whom these startling new pictures reached the public domain: Mr Robert Macrae who has done so much in recent years to popularise the colourful past of the Highlands." Robert smiled at the camera, by far the most convincing smile so far, but managing to convey acute embarrassment.

["By far the best looking!" said his wife. "But you should've had your hair cut!"]

After a pause for the inevitable polite applause from an obedient studio audience, Jason Salmon turned to the first of his guests.

"Sir Montague, if I may turn to you first, I believe you have decided views about these pictures?"

"My dear Jason, its all been great fun, but don't you think you should come clean now? It's all terribly well done, but clearly a hoax! Was it the BBC special effects department? I am sure it would take in most people, but did you see the legs on that third skeleton? My guess is that someone must have accidentally shut a van door on one of your props! Did you ever see bones angled like that? Only some terrible injury and no bone-setter around could have produced anything that shape. Then there were the shots of the so-called gold coins! Everyone conveniently out of focus so you can't read anything on them. My guess is they're gold wrapped chocolates and a computer-enhanced rendering of them inscription would be either 'Rowntrees' or 'Cadburys'." [Sniggers from captive studio audience]. "And all that dust on everything! How corny! I can only admire their restraint in not introducing a whole lot of synthetic spider webs." [More sniggers]. Sir Montague smirked in a self-satisfied way directly into the nearest camera.

Jason Salmon looked slightly uncomfortable but was far too experienced a broadcaster to be seriously upset.

"The BBC received this material from the Museum Archivist and I can assure you that the Corporation had nothing whatever to do with its production."

"Did the Archivist happen to notice the date on the post-mark? Was it by any chance 1st April? Perhaps ITV has been having you on? Very well done, I say, but not quite good enough!" The smug baronet settled back in his chair and the obsequious audience applauded.

When the applause subsided, Salmon turned to the younger of his two female guests.

"Mrs Grant, may I ask, do you share Sir Montague's opinion? Is this an elaborate hoax, or the genuine article?"

Adjusting her skirt to reveal an extra inch or two of hefty thigh, Mrs Grant smiled directly at the camera.

"Indeed I do not!" Her accent was a contrived mixture of West Highland and North American. "These valuable pictures have been examined by some of Scotland's leading historians.

"Admittedly Sir Montague is not alone in his views. However, the overwhelming opinion of the people who really know about these things..." [At this Sir Montague gave her a glare that should have made her curl up and die but seemed to bounce harmlessly off her.] "....is that these are authentic illustrations that capture something of the drama of the fascinating era of Scottish history in the mid-18th century. It is now of the utmost importance that the person who took these photos be identified and encouraged to lead an expedition of a selected team of scientists and historians to investigate thoroughly and to produce an authoritative report that will silence sensation-seeking critics for good." [Sir Montague glowered even more savagely, were that possible]. "I, for one, think that a new special graveyard should be consecrated on the battle-field of Culloden and the poor casualties of those sad times be given a proper Christian burial."

Before Jason Salmon could reply, a bad-tempered Sir Montague butted in,

"My dear lady," he began pompously.

"I am not your 'dear lady', or anyone else's, for that matter," she snapped tartly.

Ignoring her completely, the baronet continued,

"I am sure you will find that the photographer will prove to be rather elusive. Nor will you find any cave. It does not exist. The nearest thing you may find is a well-equipped studio looking for publicity. Of course, if the BBC thinks it has egg on its face, it will be keen to suppress the whole business. Just wait and see!"

"Rubbish!" The woman on his right was clearly furious. "This kind of criticism is totally unjustified. This is a serious historical matter and is not to be dismissed from serious consideration by prejudiced bigots, even if they do enjoy a title!"

Her anger was clearly infectious and the little man was now bouncing up and down in his seat trying to get a word in. The suave Jason Salmon intervened urbanely but firmly, silencing the spluttering Sir Montague before he could get started again.

"Clearly, there is more than one opinion represented here and I would at this point like to ask Mr Robert Macrae through whose hands the pictures were passed to the Archives for his opinion. First, to clear the ground, Mr Macrae, have you the slightest doubt as to the authenticity of this material?"

Looking straight into the camera, but appearing to be replying directly to the chairman, Robert spoke with evident conviction.

"These films were sent to me by a very respectable historian. I recognised their importance and passed them on to the Archivists because I knew they made an important contribution to our pool of data on that era. I have since been able to confirm that the historian who sent these to me took the photographs personally. That person wishes to remain anonymous but I do assure you that I am speaking of someone of the highest integrity, utterly incorruptible and with no axe to grind."

["Well said, Robert!" said Mary].

Turning to his fourth guest, Salmon asked,

"Professor McAskill, may I turn to you now? Has this material impressed you as being authentic?"

"Of course, one would have to visit the site itself to be really sure. However, one has made a detailed study of enlarged prints, concentrating on the weapons and the other artefacts. Without data about humidity and the water content of the environment in which these items are alleged to have been stored for 250 years, it is not possible for one to be absolutely sure. However, one might be persuaded of their authenticity but one could only be sure beyond a peradventure if one could make one's own study aided by one's own staff."

"One might think it authentic then?" asked Jason. [The wretched woman's got me doing the 'one thinks this or one thinks that' thing myself, he thought with self-contempt].

"Indeed one does. One could only really be sure if one were afforded the opportunity of a scientific examination, but on the basis of the available data, the answer one would arrive at might well be affirmative."

Jason Salmon blinked. He thought the professor was saying 'Yes', but, wilting under the barrage of verbiage, he backed off. Swinging round on his chair, he addressed the other lady guest.

"Mrs Grant, I would like to come back to you, if I may. The matter of the gold coins. Leaving aside for the moment the question of whether these pictures are authentic or not, from your study of this period in Scottish history, does it seem

129

likely that large quantities of bullion might be floating around the Highlands?"

"It's well documented that the French did fund the Jacobite rebellion. However, this has not been my area of speciality. I'm sure that either of the two gentlemen could speak with more authority than I can." She smiled sweetly at Robert on her right and glowered with ill-concealed dislike at Sir Montague on her left.

Jason turned to Robert,

"Mr Macrae, a pile of gold like that in the picture" [On a screen above the panel's heads the best of the blurred 'coins' photos appeared.] "would represent a fortune now, never mind 250 years ago. In a poverty-stricken Scotland after 18 months of strife: fact or fiction?"

Robert was in his element. He had made a detailed study of the period and knew his subject.

"It is indeed well-documented that the French sent gold to finance the Uprising, as I am sure Sir Montague will confirm." [The baronet nodded vigorously, secretly glad to be able to agree with someone at last]. "Just after the defeat at Culloden, substantial quantities of gold coins were landed on the west coast. Most of it disappeared, but there is little doubt that it was landed. Wouldn't you agree, Sir Montague?"

"Indeed," came the reply, "it was handed over to Cameron of Lochiel and others and has never really surfaced since. The most convincing accounts suggest that Cameron and his brother buried on their lands near Loch Arkaig."

"But they presumably dug it up again," interjected the chairman. "It would not just be left there, surely?"

"Well, that remains a mystery," continued Sir Montague. "What we do know is that both Ewan Cameron and his brother, Dr Archibald Cameron were caught and executed by the Government forces. Indeed, Archibald has the dubious distinction of being the last British subject to be hung, drawn and quartered, but that is another matter. What is clear is that neither lived to enjoy what must have by any standards amounted to a king's ransom. The other leading characters that history puts at or near the scene are Lord Lovat and Cluny McPherson. Lovat lost his head at Tower Hill, the last British subject to be beheaded, incidentally. That leaves McPherson. He lived as a fugitive on his ancestral lands for several years before going to France where he died in poverty."

"A very good summary, if I may say so, Sir Montague," added Robert. "Even if someone else had got their hands on the money, no-one could start spending that kind of money, particularly French gold coins, in 18th century Scotland and not be noticed. The amount of money involved is subject to debate. It did exist, though. The most likely scenario is that it was buried and the secret of where died with the Cameron brothers. It's somewhere near Loch Arkaig and the Cameron castle at Achnacarry."

"So we all get our metal-detectors and head for Loch Arkaig, then, do we?" smiled Jason Salmon.

"I think not," replied the baronet. "We've been overtaken by more recent history. A later, 20th century, Lord Lovat and several thousand commandos trained in that area in the last war. They were playing for keeps and much of the training was done with live ammunition. Scratch the surface anywhere within ten miles of Achnacarry and all you'll get is cartridge cases, shell fragments and spent bullets!"

"I knew Achnacarry rang a bell somewhere," said Salmon. He had had the feeling that control over the direction of the debate had been slipping from him and was anxious to stamp his authority on the proceedings. "Suppose, just suppose, at least some of this gold was recovered, whose would it be?"

"Treasure Trove!" said Robert promptly. "It would go to the Crown, with a suitable reward for the finder."

"So why has your correspondent not claimed it, if it exists?" chimed in Sir Montague triumphantly. "Either he's keeping it all for himself or he can't hand it over because it isn't there!"

"Or is totally unmotivated by money," said Robert mildly.

The professor clearly felt she had been silent too long.

"One notices that you scrupulously use language that is gender-neutral. May one therefore assume your correspondent is of the female gender?"

Robert replied, "That would be an unwarranted assumption. Indeed, you might think it more likely that a man would be exploring caves than a woman."

"So it was a woman!" The professor was jubilant.

Salmon intervened, "Mr Macrae did not actually say that, professor. Now, may I ask you what you think should be done with this treasure if, eventually, it is discovered?"

"One feels it should be used for the good of those who suffered as a result of the suppression of the Highlands."

"And how do we identify them? Aren't we simply 200 years too late," asked Salmon with a smile.

"Well, their descendants, then. The families of the victims of oppression, both the oppression following the '45 and that of the evictions of the clearances."

"So many of the oppressed emigrated," said Mrs Grant, glad that the subject was veering in the direction of her pet interests. "The trouble is, how can anyone redress the injustices of the past? So many Scots were evicted from grounds their forebears had tilled for centuries. Evicted because they had no written charter to give them title to their traditional lands. But, having been evicted by means of writs and bailiffs, they went off to the Americas and promptly evicted the native Indians with muskets and pistols. These Indians, too, had no written title to their lands. Their descendants suffer still. Do we compensate them?"

["A brave lady. She won't make friends back home if she speaks out like that. But she's got a point, you must admit," muttered McPherson.]

The professor looked uncomfortable and, for once, short on words. Robert came to her rescue.

"We have, I'm afraid, to accept humbly that we cannot redress the many social injustices of the past. All we can do is to try to learn from them and seek to ensure that we, in our generation, work for a fairer society. We can no more compensate the descendants of the oppressed of former centuries than we can punish today's generation for crimes their forebears committed. We learn from the past, but we must also let go of the past. If we obsessively dwell on the terrible things that happened in former years, the bitterness this will create will destroy our happiness. When the gold is found, I would like to see it used for the common good of the whole of Britain, making it a symbol of unity rather than of division."

The debate went on for a further ten minutes, becoming increasingly diffuse. By the time the programme concluded, the subject had been explored and exhausted.

Chapter 6

Back in the Macraes' comfortable lounge, the three friends relaxed in a companionable atmosphere, mellowed by the now empty bottle of wine.

"You were great, Robert," said his wife with unconcealed pride. "I loved the way that you only had to hint that the photos were taken by a man for that wretched woman to assume it was a woman!"

"Thanks for that," said McPherson. "It was a useful smoke-screen. I don't think it'll help much, however. Too many reporters know where the film was developed. Sooner or later, I must go home and face the music! What a fool I was taking those photographs!"

"It's my fault for publishing them," replied Robert contritely. "Worse still, I've made money out of it. I was paid £350 for that TV appearance! Now ITV want to interview both Sir Montague and me. They don't know that I can't stand that self-satisfied, opinionated little twit!"

Chapter 7

Anxious not to overstay his welcome, McPherson decided to curtail his visit to Edinburgh and to return to his own Speyside home. Still far from completely fit, he was nevertheless very much better and perfectly capable of fending for himself once more. His hosts were genuinely sorry to see him go, but knew better than to argue with him once his mind was made up. Both Mary and Robert went to Waverley station to see him off.

"I'll be sure to watch your TV show," he assured Robert. "Just make sure it's as entertaining as the last one and don't let Sir Montague intimidate you!"

"Don't worry! This is supposed to be a much more intellectual debate, anyway, not a wrangle about whether your photos are forgeries. The emphasis is on the French involvement in the '45. Sir Montague and I probably have less to fight about on that subject."

"A pity!" The older man looked positively disappointed. "I was looking forward to you having a real fight on your hands! Don't make it too tame or they won't ask you back!"

At that the whistle blew and the train started its journey northwards. Three hours later, it pulled into the little station at Kingussie. McPherson alighted and was grateful to find a taxi in the station yard. Ten minutes later he was home. Soon the kettle was boiling and he felt he could relax. Then the door-bell rang. Two reporters were there and soon an auction of offers from two rival newspapers assailed his ears. Politely, but very firmly, he declined all their overtures and shut the door. However, there was to be no peace. The phone rang - another reporter, another paper and another offer! When the call ended, he took the receiver off the hook. He could do that with the telephone, but taking the battery out of the door-bell only led to loud knocking. By evening he felt exhausted.

Just as he finished his evening meal, there was another bang on the door. Wearily he staggered over to open it, ready with his stock refusal to talk to any reporter, a refusal that was now blunt to the point of rudeness. It was not the press this time. It was the police, the local bobby and an impressively large colleague whose stripes proclaimed he was a sergeant.

"Heard you were back," said Grant. "We want a word. May we come in, please?" The question was polite enough but it was more of a demand than a request. McPherson stood aside and waved the two officers into his sitting room. They were so big that, though there were only the two of them, the little room looked seriously over-crowded. It was only slightly better when they had all sat down.

"Now about these bodies, Mr McPherson," said Grant, a man who liked to come to the point quickly. "We have to investigate any unexplained deaths and give a report to the procurator fiscal. I can understand you not wanting to tell the press where they are, but you will have to tell us."

"Now what bodies would these be?" asked McPherson innocently.

"Don't play with us," cut in the sergeant abruptly. "They may have been dead for years, but they still have to be investigated."

"Would these be the bodies on that TV programme," asked McPherson, still in his most naive voice. "Why come to me?"

"You know fine," said Grant, "as does every reporter in the land. You sent the film for developing. We've traced it and there's no good denying it."

"I may have had a film developed right enough, but surely that's not against the law, is it?"

The sergeant was not pleased. "We can charge you with concealing a death, or rather, seven deaths. And we will if you continue to obstruct us."

"Oh, I'm not wanting to obstruct you, but I think you can safely assume that anyone born more than 200 years ago is dead now. So why waste your time?"

"It's you that's wasting police time, and we can charge you with that, too." The sergeant was now quite angry.

"I didn't come bothering you, so I don't think you can say I've wasted your time. Looking into things which happened a couple of centuries ago - now that sounds like a waste of your time."

"Right, Grant. Charge him with concealing seven deaths!" The sergeant was reaching boiling point.

Another innocent smile from McPherson. "I don't think it will stick," he said. "Sir Montague Fraser and no doubt several other expert witnesses will testify that the pictures were fakes done in a studio."

"So, you admit to false pretences, then? Grant! Caution him and charge him with that."

Grant pulled out a notebook, but before he had even started on the caution, the old man replied. "I have not asked for any money. I have not been paid anything. So how will a charge of false pretences stick? Besides, the learned Professor McAskill and others will testify that the pictures are genuine."

Grant tried not to smile. The sergeant didn't look as though he ever smiled and certainly was not going to start now. "You're trying to be too clever. We must have an answer so you'll just have to make up your mind to tell us. All right," he said in an effort to be conciliatory, "I know you're only just back home and barely settled in. We'll leave it for now. Sleep on it. Constable Grant will be round for a statement tomorrow." He rose, and the two officers left.

Outside they sat in the police car.

"The trouble is, we can't really force him," said the sergeant. "If we lean on him at all, there will be howls about police harassment. The press are all over Speyside and they're playing this story for all it's worth. That McPherson is a cunning old bird! I'll speak to the Procurator, but I think it may be that you'll be too busy tomorrow to follow this up!

Chapter 8

With a vague feeling that he had won the verbal skirmish, but would lose the war, McPherson went to bed. The next morning he had to restock his larder. With only slight doubt, he turned the key in his ageing Morris Minor. It had not turned a wheel since that fateful day back in April. Nevertheless, it started obediently. Had he been more attentive to his rear-view mirror, he might have noticed a large black Jeep pull out and follow him into Kingussie. Kingussie was, as usual, so quiet that he was able to park right outside the general store. The Jeep slid into a parking place several yards down the street.

Twenty minutes later, having bought all his supplies, exchanged gossip with three or four old friends and parried the questions of the loquacious shop-keeper, he loaded his purchases into his car. A well-built stranger sauntered up. Another reporter, he thought. After a second glance, he revised this opinion. He was already getting good at recognising reporters at a hundred yards. The man stopped.

"Lovely cars, the Minors. Had one myself, my very first car. Never let me down. Have you had yours long?"

Disarmed, and relieved that this was all the stranger wanted to talk about, McPherson finished putting his packages in the car and straightened up.

"I bought it new in 1967. I'd had a 1955 one before that and, I suppose because I don't really like change, I went for the same thing, although, of course, this has a bigger engine, disc brakes and whatnot. Still, it's essentially the same car and I like it. I've done 125,000 miles and, apart from regular servicing, I've spent nothing on it. That's why I hang on to it. You know, better the devil you know and all that." It was nice to talk to someone who was interested in anything at all which had nothing to do with that wretched cave.

The stranger replied, "Mine was one of the first with the 1000cc engine. No disc brakes then, of course. I must admit I had a few exciting moments in it. Not the car's fault, just youthful optimism well mixed with lack of experience! Why I didn't roll it, I'll never know! The engines are nearly indestructible. I drove the poor thing as if it was a racing car, screaming round corners on two wheels! You know, just the daft things teenagers do until they get hurt or they mature a bit, whichever comes first!"

"And what do you drive now?" McPherson asked.

"Oh, a Ford Mondeo. Company car, of course. Wouldn't be my first choice, but the boss pays the bills so he chooses the car! Mustn't complain! Nice talking to you, but I'd better press on."

And off he went, and McPherson thought no more about it. Nice chap. Friendly Glasgow accent. No more to it than that.

Chapter 9

That evening he settled down to watch the Robert Macrae/ Sir Montague Fraser interview. The chairman, the well-known ITV personality, David Thomson, introduced the two guests.

"The tremendous upsurge in interest in the Jacobite Rebellion of 1745 and the way Bonnie Prince Charlie was funded has been nearly unprecedented. Every section of the media has been involved and there has been much speculation on the part that France played in seeking to destabilise the British Government of the day." [Can't bring himself to admit that it all stems from a BBC broadcast, however, thought McPherson]. "Tonight we have Sir Montague Fraser and Mr Robert Macrae, both acknowledged experts in this tempestuous time in our Nation's history. Although not sharing the same opinion about some of the more controversial material that has been bandied about in recent weeks," [A real dig at the BBC, that one, the old man thought]. "these two scholars have between them published over twenty papers on Prince Charles Edward Stewart, the Young Pretender or Bonnie Prince Charlie, depending on your point of view." Thomson gave one of his famous smiles directly at the camera.

"Now, Robert Macrae, may I turn first to you. Was France really involved in the 1745 rebellion or was it more of a England versus Scotland thing altogether?"

"Before we go a step further," replied Robert, "we really must make clear that the Jacobite rebellions were not a war between Scotland and England. It is true that the Highland chiefs, in the main, supported Prince Charles. Their clans followed their chiefs, without regard for the beliefs of the individual clansman. There was some support for the Jacobite cause in the Lowlands too, as also in England. However, we should not lose sight of the fact that many Scots, including some of the Highland clans, fought on the Government side. Did you know, for instance, that six Scottish regiments fought for King George at Culloden? However, back to your question about French intervention.

"France had been involved much more heavily in the years immediately prior to the '45. A year earlier, an army of over 10,000 men set off to assist the Highland clans in an uprising. They were beaten back, partly by the British Navy but more by bad weather. By 1745 however, the French will to support the Jacobite cause had largely gone."

"This country owes a tremendous debt to Fleury. Wouldn't you agree?" asked Sir Montague, directing his question to Robert, who looked puzzled for a few seconds, then light seemed to dawn on his face.

"Indeed, you're right! I've never thought of it like that! There should be a statue in his memory in Westminster Abbey. The British Empire owes him a tremendous debt of gratitude!"

"Oh, no! Fleury was a Roman Catholic Cardinal. I hardly think he'd like to be remembered in an Anglican Church!"

The two television guests were obviously enjoying a private joke and David Thomson and nearly every viewer felt left out. Slightly miffed, he asked.

"Fleury? Who was he? I can't say I remember the name. Who was he?"

Robert replied, "Cardinal Fleury was the tutor of King Louis of France and, when Louis came to the throne, became his principle advisor. He had a genius for foreign policy. Indeed, he was the nearest thing France had to a foreign secretary in those days."

"But what did he do to benefit the British Empire?" asked a still puzzled Thomson.

"He died!" replied Sir Montague laconically. Thomson now looked totally flummoxed, so the baronet went on. "You explain, Macrae. You're much better at this than I am."

Surprised, flattered and almost unwillingly warming to the little man, Robert picked up the theme. "The 17th Century was the most crucial time for all the would-be empires and emperors. France and Britain were competing in the Americas, particularly in Canada, in Africa and in India. Cardinal Fleury had the vision to recognise that a Britain torn apart by wars at home would be unable to secure an empire abroad. But he died in 1744, a year before Prince Charlie's rebellion. Had he been still in a position to influence French foreign policy, the whole of European and, indeed, world history would have been different.

"Fortunately, Louis and his advisors in 1745 did not have Fleury's breadth of vision. If they had supported Prince Charles from the word go, the next 50 years of British history would have been marked by civil war. Instead, the French sent too little help, and what it did send was too late to influence the outcome. Culloden had been fought and lost before the first significant French contribution of arms and gold arrived. Now, if Prince Charles had been supported adequately from the beginning, he would have advanced on London, instead of turning back at Derby."

"And we would have had a Jacobite Royal Family as a result?" asked David Thomson.

"Not necessarily, but we would certainly have had a prolonged period of unrest, if not outright civil war, and that was all France needed. If Britain had been distracted by conflicts at home, it would never have won India and Canada, both of which were brought into the British Empire within 15 years of Culloden and both of which were won from the French."

"And, incidentally, both won by British Armies with substantial Scottish regiments in their make-up," added Sir Montague.

"So the French might have had the Empire on which the sun never set?" asked Thomson, really interested by now.

Sir Montague continued, "It was certainly within their grasp. If Fleury had been there to advise, who knows? There might have been no French Revolution. Louis' family might have escaped the guillotine!"

"I'm not so sure about that," said Robert. "The grievances that led to the French Revolution ran very deep. What I do think is that a Britain, weakened by years of civil strife and with a negligible empire, would have fallen to Napoleon. There would have been no Trafalgar and no Waterloo, or else they would have been French victories. The whole of Europe would have been under French dominion as well as the greater part of what was the British Empire."

"Fascinating! So we should all give three cheers for Fleury and his timely death?" said Thomson.

"Re-writing history is great fun, but totally speculative," added Sir Montague. "If Napoleon had won, the German states would never have been forged into the German nation. At the price of being ruled from Paris, we might have escaped two world wars. I can't say I like the idea of being ruled by Paris but we're increasingly ruled from Brussels and seem to be able to live with that!"

Back at his Speyside home, McPherson had been enthralled. The debate was entirely different from what he, or anyone else had expected. The gold had not been mentioned and that could only be a good thing. He went to bed happy and relaxed. However, the next day would change all that.

Chapter 10

About ten the next morning, there was a knock at the cottage door. Opening it, McPherson was surprised to find his Morris Minor enthusiast friend from yesterday smiling there. Without pausing to wonder how the man knew where he lived, he courteously invited him in for coffee.

"My name's Morton, by the way, James Morton, but please call me Jim."

"Mine's McPherson. Mr McPherson to those who don't know me well. Plain McPherson to my friends. No one uses my first name, so, McPherson to you."

Morton picked up where the conversation of the day before had ended and for an enjoyable ten minutes or more the two chatted about the virtues and vices of Morris Minors. Then, Morton burst his bombshell.

"What I've really come about is a business proposition. My boss, David Raven, has asked me to negotiate terms with you. We know you can't get the gold out and market it by yourself. Everything you do is being watched too closely by the media. Besides, you won't have the contacts. Now, this is where Mr Raven can help. He knows how to get things done and he has contacts, not just in Scotland, mind you, but world-wide. We can spirit the gold away under the very noses of the press, turn it into sterling, dollars or whatever you want and no one will be the wiser. All we need is for you to take us once to the place. We'll do the rest. All you would then do is to sit at home and wait for us to drop the cash in. Of course, as we would be doing the work and taking the risks, we would need a decent cut. How does 20% to you and 80% to us sound?"

McPherson was appalled. For over a minute he could barely draw a breath, let alone speak. He tried to find words to express his contempt but his incoherent splutter was misunderstood, perhaps deliberately.

"I tried to tell Mr Raven that 20/80 wasn't good enough, but he's a hard man to deal with. I think he'd go to 30/70. Would you like me to try him?" At this the visitor started to pull out a mobile phone. The old man found his voice.

"Indeed you will not. Whatever kind of a man do you think I am? You'll just be getting out of here and you can tell your Mr Raven that the answer 'No' and will go on being 'No'. I'm never going back to that cave, with you or anyone else! And as for the suggestion that I join you in what is a criminal conspiracy, well, words fail me!"

He was on his feet now, shaking partly with shock and partly with righteous indignation. Morton rose. As he walked to the door, he said sadly,

"Such a pity. Mr Raven will not be pleased. I remember once before when he was not pleased. The other chap had such a run of bad luck after that! A terrible accident, both legs broken! Very sad! Never really able to walk again properly. However, accidents will happen. You know how it is!"

"Don't you dare threaten me!" McPherson's blood was really up now. "Get out and stay away from me!"

After Morton had left, he sank into his chair, covered in a cold sweat and trembling all over. It was several minutes before he recovered his composure. What should he do? If the police had been more friendly, he might have contacted them. As it was, it would be nearly as humiliating to ask the help of that sergeant as to give in to Morton and the mysterious Mr Raven. He could slip away to Edinburgh. That would provide a breathing space but no permanent solution. Besides he might be followed. The thought of in any way bringing trouble to Robert and Mary was enough to make him forget the idea. He could just sit tight. There was no real risk of them maiming or killing him. He alone could lead them to their coveted prize. They wouldn't dare put him out of action. Two cups of coffee later, and he had convinced himself. He would call their bluff, sit tight and do nothing.

The following two days passed uneventfully, but in the late evening of the third day, there was a knock at the door. Morton was back and, with him a florid, overweight man in his mid-fifties. This time there was no invitation to enter. The two barged in, forcing the old man back until the backs of his knees met the edge of his chair. A firm hand pushed his chest and he sat down abruptly.

"Mr Morton will have explained what I want. He should also have explained that I am not offering you an alternative. He has been far too generous in suggesting a 30/70 split and

I'm annoyed about that." Morton looked distinctly uncomfortable. "The deal is 20/80 and that is that."

Wearily McPherson said, "There is no deal, and that's that! I'm an old man and I've lived quite long enough. I need neither money nor do I care if you shorten the remainder of my life. Do your worst, but I'll not co-operate with bandits like you."

"Stirring stuff! No doubt you feel very heroic and brave! If you change your mind, meet us at the bird sanctuary car park tomorrow morning at eight." And at this, the two unwanted visitors headed for the door. McPherson was puzzled. What was their game? What would be their next move? He did not have to wait long. Putting his hand on the door-knob, Raven turned.

"To change the subject completely, I met your nephew's daughter. Katrina, isn't it? At Bristol University doing art, isn't she? Lovely girl! I was awfully taken with her. That blond hair! A real looker!"

The old man's blood ran cold. Did this reptile's tentacles stretch the length and breadth of the whole country? The suave voice continued.

"Reminded me of a lassie I once knew in Glasgow. Another real beauty! But she and I didn't get on. Terrible thing happened to her. Acid. They never caught the man who threw it in her face. So sad, a lovely little kid like that. The acid burnt so deep that it destroyed the tissues below the skin. So skin-grafts were impossible. She looked terrible, not that she ever saw herself in a mirror. The acid got her eyes too. Isn't it shocking what can happen to an innocent, wee lassie! But there it is! We live in a dreadful world, don't we?

150

However, mustn't keep you. Good night. Oh, and by the way, you won't forget, will you? The bird sanctuary at eight? We'll let ourselves out. Goodnight!"

McPherson was shattered. His heart was pounding almost audibly. His body shook uncontrollably. Icy trickles of sweat ran down his spine. What could he do? The police? But with no witnesses and no evidence? They could not touch Raven and Morton. Oh, they no doubt could pull them in and grill them. But what then? A good lawyer and the pair would be out within an hour. Then what? The police, even supposing they believed him, could watch his niece for a month or two, but not for ever.

Chapter 11

It was dark in the little cottage before McPherson moved from his chair. He had weighed and considered every conceivable course of action open to him. Stubborn though he was, he knew he was beaten, unless, of course, he was prepared to gamble with his niece's safety. Sadly he thought, if only I were thirty years younger! His dimly-remembered unarmed combat training would have ensured that the two would not have left the cottage alive. But not now. He was but a pale shadow of the man who had fought in the Eighth Army under Montgomery. There had been a time when he could have taken out those two and they would not have known what hit them, but not now. The only safe course was to go along with them and worry about getting justice later.

He staggered off to bed, feeling absolutely drained. Sleep was elusive. Would he even make it up the hill? It would be no great tragedy if he did not and the two rogues were left to ponder that they had killed their own chosen goose before they saw a single golden egg. Then came the thought, could they afford to let him come down alive? Probably not. Into the small hours he tossed and turned. Every strategy he could think of was fraught with danger, not to himself alone, that would have been acceptable, but to Katrina. Eventually he did sleep, but only fitfully. By six o'clock he was wide awake but anything but refreshed. All he could do was to bide his time and be alert to any developing situation that might provide a way forward.

At quarter to eight, his Morris pulled up at the deserted bird sanctuary. Five minutes later, a rather sinister black Jeep growled in alongside his car. He wound down his window. Raven climbed out of the passenger seat of the Jeep and strolled insolently over.

"Good to see you, Mr McPherson. Nice enough now, but it looks like rain later. No! Stay where you are! We'll take your car. On second thoughts, Morton can drive. We don't want any accidents, do we?"

The man's a mind reader, thought McPherson. He'd been wondering if he would have the courage to drive off into a convenient ravine or to wrap his poor old car round some suitable pine tree. The trouble is, now that all cars have seatbelts, you cannot guarantee the results. Reluctantly he got out and opened the back door.

"You'll be more comfortable in the front seat. I'll be right behind you, so you won't be lonely."

What I'd give to wipe that smile off his face, the old man thought, reluctantly sitting in the front passenger seat. As he did so, he observed that both men were wearing gloves, despite it being a warm summer morning. Now he knew they did not intend him to return from the cave.

"Morton's a good driver," purred Raven. "Just give him clear instructions and we'll all get along just fine."

There was no real alternative but to obey. The little car crossed the valley again and was soon grinding its way in first gear up a seldom used track that penetrated deep into the Mondaliath Mountains. It took fully an hour to cover only slightly more than four miles. The track ended at a small stand of Scots Pine. Morton reversed in among the trees and switched off the engine. The three men got out in silence. Morton swung a substantial pack on his shoulder. McPherson picked up his much smaller haversack. Raven had quite enough of a burden if he just carried his substantial mid-riff up the mountain track. They set off, McPherson in front, setting a slow but steady pace he knew he could maintain. After only half an hour, the two city men were perspiring freely and Raven called a halt. He pulled out a gold cigarette case and was soon puffing away. Morton followed suit. McPherson ate a chocolate bar. The sky was becoming more overcast and Raven's prophecy of rain looked increasingly accurate.

"Right, said Raven, throwing away the stub end of his cigarette. "Let's get on. How much farther to go?"

"About seven miles, three hours at this rate. I'll go faster if you like," said McPherson, helpful only because he knew the other two were already finding the going tough. Doubtless the obviously new boots they wore were not helping either man. Increasingly, McPherson felt he was in his element and the other pair were clearly getting farther and farther from theirs. An hour and three more stops later, the rain came, not torrential, but that fine, wetting, persistent rain that truly deserves the description 'highland rain'. It did nothing for the spirits of his companions and McPherson only welcomed it because he thought that it troubled them even more than it troubled him. The path became steeper and less well defined. Raven was toiling and becoming more and more suspicious.

"If you're leading us on a wild goose chase, believe me, you'll be sorry, but not half so sorry as that niece of yours will be. How far now?"

"You see that point with the rocks up there ahead? There's a waterfall there. We skirt up round it, on for another half mile until we reach a lochan, then up the scree-slope and we're there."

Morton looked mutinous, struggling as he was under the huge rucksack. Only greed for gold kept him loyal and kept him going.

The track was now almost non-existent. Lack of sleep, allied with his recent illness, was catching up on the old man. He felt light-headed and it took him all his strength to keep going. A heart attack now might be the best thing, he thought, as long as it's a fatal one. Raven looked a much more likely candidate for cardiac arrest. His body ached every limb and he was now powered almost exclusively by the strength of his obstinate will. The three stumbled past the cataract, reaching the more level ground of the corrie above. To the right were steep hills that even a fit man would struggle up. To the left were formidable precipitous slopes, sheer cliffs skirted by rough scree-slopes that were made up of small rocks interspersed with some of car-size boulders. McPherson led them at a snail's pace up through the larger rocks until they were walking precariously on a rabbit-track at the very foot of the cliff. At last, clearing the stones from the hole at the base of the cliff, he said, "There! And this is as far as I go." He shuffled off his pack and sat down.

Raven was puffing and panting. The final approach up the scree-slope had very nearly finished him.

"No way!" he said. "You're coming with us. If you think we're dropping down that hole and leaving you here, you've another think coming."

Reluctantly, McPherson opened his haversack. He took out his rope and fixed round the same rock as he had used on his last visit. He pulled out his torch and gently eased himself into the darkness below. Next came Morton, closely followed by his rucksack which Raven had forced through the hole after him. Morton dragged out a large torch, lit it and placed it in a cranny between two projecting rocks. The torch was followed by two butane lanterns. Once these were lit, the cave was reasonably well-illuminated. Morton paled visibly as he turned and found the two sightless eyes of the first skull staring directly at him. Meanwhile, above, to the accompaniment of a barrage of curses, Raven was struggling to get his excessive bulk through the opening to the cave. He lost his grip on the rope and arrived ignominiously in a cascade of shingle at the feet of the other two. He pulled himself up, looking not a little shaken.

"So this is it, then," he said, picking up one of the lanterns and examining the nearest skeleton. Raven clearly felt none of the squeamishness that his accomplice did. He stirred the dust with his foot. A large oval stone rolled out of the debris around the recumbent skeletal remains. He picked it up, looked at it and dropped it at his feet. McPherson's interest was aroused. He waited for the other two to move deeper into the cave. He then stooped and picked up the stone. There was something engraved on it. The old man rubbed it on his sleeve and looked again. He could make out nothing but a few scratches, man-made clearly. Despite the circumstances, he could not restrain his curiosity. It might be interesting so he slipped it into his anorak pocket. He looked round. The much-improved light revealed the crumbling remains of fire-lock pistols, muskets and even a genuine blunderbuss.

Chapter 12

Meanwhile, Raven and Morton had found the gold. Morton held the light while Raven clambered down the steep rock into the lower recesses of the cave. He reached up and took the lantern from Morton. McPherson had now been completely forgotten. Morton emptied the rucksack, dropped it at Raven's feet and scrambled down. Both stood, awe-struck, gazing at the cone of coins at their feet. Raven stooped and ran his fingers through the heavy discs, scattering a cloud of dust as he did. He choked, suddenly breathless, and stood up again. His head swam and he swayed slightly. In this deeper section of the cave, the air was even more foul than above. The cocktail of gases from the fire and the lamp, both of which went out 250 years earlier, still filled this lower chamber. Leaning on the rocky wall, Raven reached for his cigarette case. In a rare show of generosity, he offered one to Morton. The two men drew the smoke into their lungs. They had done it! They had won! Before them lay the prize and they relished the moment.

McPherson had had enough. He was conscious of being short of breath. His chest was beginning to hurt. The other two were now on their knees, pre-occupied with scooping up the coins and packing them in the rucksack. Quietly, he crept to the foot of the slope, grasped the rope and scrambled up into the daylight and the pure fresh air above. Never had he been so glad to feel the rain falling on his head. However, his absence was noted. Raven stood up suddenly with a cry. Then, his head swimming, he keeled over, banging his head on a projecting rock as he did so. It is a feature of head injuries that they bleed copiously. Morton gazed in horror at the rapidly spreading pool of blood round his employer's head. He looked up, wondering where his duty lay. Should he chase and bring the old guy back? Or should he stay and do what he could for Raven? Not that he liked the older man. He feared and detested him. But Raven had the contacts. Raven always knew what to do next. Raven had never been caught. He, Morton, had never been in prison since joining Raven. So he stayed. He bent down and tried to stop the bleeding. Raven moaned but did not regain consciousness. Morton was finding it difficult to think. His head was swimming. He tried to stand, but his legs were like jelly. He sank back beside Raven and slumped on the rucksack. He gasped for air and, for several minutes the sound of his laboured breathing was the only noise in the cave. His only motion was his heaving chest. Then that stopped and there was only a silence, a deathly silence.

Chapter 13

Gradually his breathing became easier and McPherson started to think more clearly. He must put distance between himself and the two thugs. He thought for a fleeting second of trying to seal the cave mouth but dismissed the idea. Any rock he could move to cover the entrance would be easily dislodged by the combined efforts of the two men below. Flight was the only answer. Flight, and the strong possibility that, having got the gold, the two would rapidly lose interest in him. Although Raven was twenty years his junior, McPherson was confident that he could outpace him. Morton was more of a problem.

Reckoning that the Glaswegians would naturally assume that he would head for his car by the most direct route, McPherson slithered along the scree, gaining height steadily. He passed a projecting buttress of rock and, knowing he was now out of sight of the cave entrance, he slowed down. His chest still hurt and his breathing was laboured. However, by cutting his speed to little over one mile an hour, he could keep going, leaving the cave behind and below. A few more hundred feet and he would cross the head of the corrie and be over the watershed into the head of the next glen. This was not a parallel glen and following it down would not take him back to his car. It would, at the cost of a few extra miles, bring him to a remote farm and to safety. He should be all right. Once over the col, it might be a featureless and trackless wilderness, but it would be downhill all the way. He should be all right for time. He had the long summer evening in which to reach the farm. The rain and accompanying mist would be more of a help than a hindrance as Morton would not spot him unless he got really close.

Comforting himself with these thoughts, McPherson soldiered on. Crossing the col took much longer than he thought. Once or twice, he thought he heard voices behind him, but there was no sign of pursuit and he decided it was highly stressed nerves misinterpreting a grouse or a pheasant. At last he was over the ridge and losing height rapidly. The heather was long and straggly. Twice he tripped and fell, but the heather that tripped him also cushioned his fall. The ground started to level out and he made his way down past a tumbling burn. Pleased with his progress, he paused and looked back. He pulled out his binoculars and raked the hillside above. Nothing stirred. They must have assumed he had headed down the route they had followed on the upward journey. Perhaps the lure of the gold had proved too much and they had not tried to chase after him. Perhaps the corpulent Raven was even now stuck in the cave mouth. The mental picture brought a wry smile to his lips.

The burn was somewhat deeper now and soon he would have to cross it, not that its depth would present any problem. Finding a suitable point he jumped on to a rock in mid-stream. It was only slightly farther to the other bank. He leapt, landed badly and slipped back into the water. If he had not been so tired, no doubt all that would have happened would have been that he would have wet feet in the shallow water. He staggered, stumbled and sat down hard in fifteen inches of water. With difficulty he clambered to his feet. He was shocked as well as thoroughly chilled. He must keep moving. At a shambling pace he pressed on down the glen. He fell more frequently now and getting up was becoming harder. A touch of cramp set in in his right thigh. He would have to stop for a rest. Beside a large rock with sufficient overhang to provide shelter from the rain, he sat down. He still had two chocolate bars, so he ate both. He tried to wring out his wet clothes but to little effect. Vigorously massaging his cramped muscle, he told himself severely that he must not give up. He must get up. He must march.

With a tremendous effort, the old man hauled himself erect. He was tottering now but still making progress. Only a few more bone-jarring miles. He did not let himself wonder about the possibility of the farmer being away from home and the place locked up and deserted. All he must concentrate on was the next few steps. His head was reeling now. The cramp was coming back. He would have to rest again. This time there was no real shelter. Miserably, he sank down beside a rock. Somehow he knew he would now never get up. Was he the man who, faced with Raven and Morton, had cocked a snoot at death, with his McBeth-like 'I have lived long enough'? He was drifting in and out of consciousness now. Part of him wanted to stay and fight. Another part wanted simply to give up, to relax and to drift away.

Chapter 14

When repeated telephone calls went unanswered, Robert and Mary became worried. It would not be possible for Robert to go north until the weekend. Mary, however was free and so she drove north, across the Forth Bridge, by-passing Perth, on up the A9 through the dramatic Drummochter Pass and on to Speyside. She reached the cottage in early afternoon. Locking doors in the Highlands is still a fairly optional course of action, one of the lingering blessings of the deeply spiritual ethos that still determines morality there. Crime in general is rare. Burglary almost unknown. It was therefore no surprise to find the door unlocked. Fearing what she might find, Mary gingerly opened the door and called out. Then with the sheepishness that everyone experiences when finding they have been addressing an empty room, she went through to the kitchen, the bedroom and, finally, the bathroom. Nothing! And nothing to cause alarm either. No signs of disturbance but no sign of McPherson. She went to the garage. The car was gone. Perhaps the police knew something. She drove to the Police Station. Only one constable was there. Mary explained her errand and her anxieties.

"Not another missing person! We're used to climbers being overdue. Happens all the time! But middle-aged and elderly men! Three in one week, well I ask you!"

"Why, who else is missing?" asked Mary.

"A couple of anglers from Glasgow. They were staying at the Duke of Gordon. Went fishing early Friday morning and haven't been seen since. They had paid a week up-front so the hotel were not too worried. We found their vehicle up in the car-park at the marshes, but no sign of them. Wife of one of them's been creating. Wants the helicopters out. The superintendent's down from Inverness. He'll sort it out."

"None of which helps me, but I do understand you're busy. If you get any word, do let me know." And, with an acute sense of having failed, she went into the village. Everyone knew McPherson but no-one had seen him since before the week-end. Nor had his car been seen.

"He has friends in Edinburgh," said the grocer comfortingly. "Probably he's staying there for a few days. He was away staying with them earlier in the month. Don't worry, that's where he'll be."

"But my husband is his friend in Edinburgh! He was staying with us but now he's disappeared." She was close to tears of worry, anger and frustration.

It is notoriously hard to induce a sense of urgency anywhere in the Highlands and if Speyside were any more laid back it would be horizontal. The rest of the day was as frustrating, and, feeling beaten, Mary headed home.

The next morning, Robert phoned the Speyside police and was put through to the superintendent.

"The weather has closed in completely here, but we have a helicopter standing by. As soon as there's a break, it will be searching the marshes. We'll get it to sweep around and see if the pilot can see a your friend's car. Needle in a haystack, though, I'm sorry to say. However, we may be lucky."

However, it was not the helicopter that found the missing Morris Minor. It was a passing bird-watcher who noticed in it the copse and mentioned it over a pint in the Star that evening. This gave direction and some sense of urgency at last to the search. Robert and Mary drove up very early on Saturday morning. The helicopter was already criss-crossing the marshes. Following directions given at the police station, they joined the superintendent in the bird sanctuary car-park from where the search was being co-ordinated.

"The man's wife has been on to the chief! Really let him have it! Between you and me, I think she thinks her husband's dead and wants to prove it. With no body, where will she be? Neither a wife nor a widow and unable to touch his money. Anyway, after the next sweep, I'm sending the chopper up the glen above where your friend's car was found. Hang around and if they radio in anything of interest, I'll let you know."

"Thanks," said Robert tersely and wandered over to where Mary was standing.

"They're flying up the glen just shortly. The superintendent says he'll let me know if they find anything of interest. That's a euphemism for if they find the poor old soul's body," he concluded dismally. There was nothing to be said and Mary slipped her arm through her husband's and said nothing.

The helicopter swung low across the marshes following the meanderings of the sluggish waters of the Spey. When it reached the point where the river enters Loch Insch, it swept away westward, climbing to follow the contour of the rapidly rising land. It disappeared from view and nothing happened for several minutes. The superintendent spoke into the radio. Robert sauntered back.

"Nothing at all, I'm afraid. I've told him to widen the search area but it's a forlorn hope. He's sweeping an area that's nearly impossibly far from the car, unless your friend was hopelessly lost. Here! Wait a minute! Something coming now!" The policemen clustered round the radio. Robert could hear the squawky voice but was too far away to make out the message. Then the superintendent came over.

"I think they've found him. Obviously dead, I'm afraid. Ground's very bad so I've told them not to try to land. We'll send in a party on foot. Too late to help your friend, so you'll understand we can't ask the pilot to take any risks."

Robert nodded sadly, not trusting himself to speak. He had liked the old man but it was only now he realised how much he really cared for him.

Chapter 15

The funeral was held a few days later. They laid him beside his wife in the little churchyard at Kincraig. Robert followed the coffin as it was carried shoulder-high to the open grave. He took a cord and, at a nod from the undertaker, helped lower it into the ground. As he did so, his eye fell on the simple brass plaque: Hamish McPherson 1919-1996. Suddenly he realised he had never known the old boy's first name. At school, it had always been 'sir'. Then, as a student, when they met it was 'Mr McPherson'. At last, at the old man's insistence, he had graduated to the close circle that called him 'McPherson'.

The police, whilst politely sympathetic, had little interest in the old man's passing. The post-mortem had confirmed death brought on by exposure and hyperthermia. The pathologist had raised only one point of interest, puzzling but not significant. The dead man's blood had a higher than expected concentration of carbon monoxide. This was not uncommon if the deceased had a defective gas appliance, but McPherson's cottage was all electric. The other explanation that his old car's exhaust system was leaking did not fit either. There were no carbon particles in his lungs. It remained one of those rather annoying loose ends that would never be tied up.

Besides, they had more pressing problems. There was still no sign of Morton and Raven and the whole thing stank. Strathclyde police reckoned Raven was a dodgy character, although they had pinned nothing on him. Morton had been jailed more than once, although not recently. Neither was known to fish, but there was no law against suddenly taking up a new sport. The fishing gear in the Jeep was all new and it was hard to say if anything were missing. Morton's Mondeo was still in the hotel car-park. There was a whisper that the two were in the Speyside to do a drugs deal. With hard drugs entering the country at any one of a thousand inlets and sea-lochs on Scotland's west coast, this was a real possibility. Perhaps the hunt for the two men or their bodies should shift away from the marshes.

Robert made a courtesy call at the police station after the funeral. The desk sergeant was courteous but clearly harassed. Robert did not linger. However, just as he was going out the door, the sergeant called him back.

"Just one thing, sir," he said. "Your old friend was a bit of a geologist, wasn't he? He had this stone in his pocket. Nothing of value but I thought you might want it. If not, we'll just throw it out."

Robert looked at it. A flat, oval stone worn smooth in a river, a few deep scratches engraved on the surface - a diagram of some sort and two or three words that might be Gaelic. Not much of a keepsake, but he slipped it into his pocket. The old fellow's legacy, he thought wryly!

"Thank you! That's very kind of you," he said and turned and walked out into the summer sunshine.